Cosmic Robotics

Morgan Drolet & Shawn Sullivan

Cover design by Andrew Charlton (Andrewinks.com)

Neon Burrito Publishing
9

IRL: Los Angeles, California
URL: Neonburrito.info

ISBN-10: 0692794239
ISBN-13: 9780692794234

Shawn Michael Sullivan

4 [currently untitled]

40 NeuroPark

61 Cotton Candy

66 Insect Fantasy

68 Nature Fantasy

70 Harold Harold Harold

73 Fractal Fiction

Morgan Christopher Drolet

80 On a Scale of One to Ten

95 Him, Her & (Cact)i

100 Laura

115 As We Dream the Sleep of Dreams

119 Orbits'

124 Dallas

135 San Juan

140 Rice & Tea

One must embrace the tapestry of life and learn to enjoy the taste of vinegar.

btw

[currently untitled]

On occasion I wish I wasn't who I am, was, or will become.

I'd rather be a hauntingly beautiful jellyfish.

And the wish is true but truth isn't a wish. Me, I'm a self-aware human on my day by day path toward death. Neither my consciousness nor my free will were my decision. This human condition has its reputation, its pros and cons and prose, anyway I've got to get this story going.

This story already lived I'm already beginning — with some oversharing — with me being me — a pinch of anxiety — but the story begins like this:

Driving across the I-15 into our Las Vegas weekend, Joel gestured toward a back seat cooler in his SUV, offered me a Guayaki Yerba Mate like his own. I accepted and smiled, felt comfortable. He smiled too. Wonderful.

I graduated high school with Joel back at Spring Valley Academy, Ohio. I hadn't seen him in the decade since his wedding in Napa Valley, California. My mental plan for seeing him again was to avoid chatting about my past ten years and everything about me, since my life in Los Angeles felt like pretty much a disaster, and I (try) only to embarrass myself in public when I want to.

What I hadn't guessed, since I'm not him, though this didn't surprise me, it delighted me, that he became very chatty about his recent life.

He was a teacher for a Seventh-day Adventist middle-school. He told me he'll soon teach high school math and physics, after taking classes to remind himself about math and physics. When not teaching he sometimes drove for Uber, bringing travelers to wineries where he was gifted drinks.

He and his wife lived in an apartment connected with a hospital where she was a nurse. He spoke of the socioeconomic reality of Napa Valley. How it was challenging for them to find a home they could buy, the area designed for the rich, not for school teachers or nurses or the larger population of immigrant workers.

He told me he and his wife wanted children but hadn't been able to have their own. They desired to foster two siblings, with adoption aspirations. On the matter of fostering before adopting, it's that adoption you pay for, while you're paid to foster. My reaction upon hearing this was *You're a great guy who would be a great dad*. Then he blossomed my impression by describing the complex nature of forming emotional relationships with children, and the possibility of parents asking for their kids back.

Sometimes Joel's parents tried to convince him to return to Wisconsin. Where he's from. Cheaper. Easier.

Not what he wanted.

This is a thing about me: I treasure hearing all of what's human.

His life sounded so healthy to me, I told him, filled with life's best nutrients, I said something like that. A job! A wife! Plans for a house! Plans for kids! Challenges yes, but fantastic plan-making. The American Dream, I remembered. People who sound as if they like themselves and their lives, when they speak to me, within the context of mutual fondness, their positivity and strength feed the resilience I often feel myself needing to make it through each day.

It's always someone else who helps me make it through

another day. As large as my perspective becomes it remains nobody's but my own. Other people are my accomplices toward giving my perspective the slip. Joel had someone else with him every day, his wife, and soon there might be kids.... this made me excited!

Joel, having listened to me marvel at his life, he clarified that during certain times he feels caged and as if his whole world is the size of his apartment. Most weekends he goes to the beach, he said, he escapes himself within the ocean. Within the ocean one can be reminded this world is bigger than one's problems. He wasn't a surfer, he was a wild flamingo. Boogie boards. His wife traveled along sometimes, and sometimes he wore beach clothes to church.

So I listened to him and still what he told me sounded way more life nourishing than finding your sorrows laid before you across lonely Los Angeles sidewalks, which was my life's presentation these days, aside from spending time with my imaginary friends while reading, writing, and working in the bookstore.

About twenty-five percent lonely sidewalks. I knew there was a lot of life but I didn't feel myself within much of it. My life needed an emotional boogie board like I can't even tell you. And Joel through telling me of his life he allowed me to ride his with him.

The SUV's radio was off. Somehow, silence never overwhelmed us.

He chatted about going to a Seventh-day Adventist teacher's convention and bumping into some of our old teachers, including Pastor Glenn, whom we remembered from our junior year. Both Joel and Pastor Glenn were new to Spring Valley Academy that year, Joel having moved to live with his uncle, prepared to enter a new school as a new person, ready to conquer his shyness, and it was a gigantic curveball to him when in the second week of school, after I returned from my one week at Bellbrook High School, which I'd guessed was a better place for me but changed my mind, during my first week back, during first-period Bible class I asked both Joel and Pastor Glenn, *How often do you masturbate?* At the time I barely knew either of them. I remembered this since Pastor Glenn had invited me to speak with him in his office that morning.

Sometimes I have to explain myself, but only fairly often. Me, I like when hard questions are easy. I like when the tough becomes friendly. I'm non-violent and I ask hard questions without wanting to punch anyone. But sometimes asking someone a hard question can make someone want to punch me, or make them want to punch themselves.

Thankfully anyway Joel was one of the most outrageous people I knew and we became tremendous friends. He was a hot spring of smiles.

We reminisced upon when, our senior year, during a series of lunch breaks we'd stolen a single Halloween ornament from a number of anonymous yards, storing our mysterious collection in Joel's Saturn until, one random day, we bestowed them upon the yard of an obscure white house.

We used the Halloween spirit to be rude, by stealing, and be kind, by surprising. *What the fuck*, we both remembered. Joel mentioned that after a week we visited the house and our decorations remained. What had the person who lived in the obscure white house wondered, we wondered. We shrugged.

This Vegas trip was my first vacation in four years. There I was outside of Los Angeles oh my god. Along the way we stopped in Primm to eat at The Mad Greek. Then we rode the Adventure Canyon Log Flume at Buffalo Bill's. For kicks. We rode it twice. Me afraid of heights, Joel recorded a video of us going down the hill our second time. I uploaded the video to Instagram. Joel uploaded a photo. We felt adventurous.

We wished everyone we knew was with us. Not really, but I'm exaggerating the feeling of being with an old friend and trying to remember the names of the twenty-two other people who had been in our graduating class. Being from a tiny school, Joel and I had been raised to care about the people we meet. Since we weren't going to meet a lot of people. This was much different than life for me in Los Angeles, where some and most days I felt nothing but random at best, and I adored metropolitan area population statistics, the large-number possibilities for shared culture and life connections, with national and international tourists even, but sometimes as a midwestern I felt the numbers press down on the city, squashing certain particulars related to caring about others. I thought there were millions of people to care about. A popular city opinion is there were too many people to care about.

Joel and I retained aspects of our midwestern friendliness and affection. Because of warmth. Isn't warmth always a bet worth making? No? I forget. Wait, I never knew. My guess is it's as *good luck* as everything else.

Joel from my past lived in my present, walked around and chatted with me. We tried to learn craps at Primm Valley Casino Resorts, but we didn't. Well, we barely did. We ventured to Whiskey Pete's. A DeLorean designed like from *Back to the Future* sat in the lobby. Joel won money in roulette through some good guesses which made us excited.

Arriving into Vegas there's some place before Vegas which looks similarish when seen from far away in a car, at least to rookies, like Joel and me, although I'd taken this drive before so when he asked *Is that Vegas?* I said *Nah there's always this place that could be Vegas but isn't*, then shortly after that and while unsure of myself I said, *Yeah but that's Vegas*, before we passed the area before Vegas which definitely isn't Vegas.

We arrived at Howard Johnson, HoJo, a clip off the strip, next to Hooters Casino Hotel. Joel had offered to pay for the two-bed room where the three of us will stay. [John, whom I'd known since sixth grade, he graduated with us, I hadn't seen him in rounded-up five years, since our goodbyes when I moved from Portland, he continuing to live outside Seattle, now with his newborn daughter, her mother, plus two sons from the mother's previous marriage... he arrives tomorrow.] Joel said he selected the cheapest hotel so he'll have more blackjack money.

I considered HoJo lovely, since I admire that which tries nothing but to exist. The feeling of trash doesn't bother me. Everything that's trash is human. *Nothing human disgusts me*. On our bathtub were brown cigarette burns. Joel noticed some of our towels arrived dirty. There was no refrigerator. And what would we do when three of us men slept in this room with two beds? Oh fuck, whatever. Over luxurious and pampered I relate best to alive and barely. I kicked my feet up on my night's bed until we ventured Downtown.

On Fremont Street Las Vegas laced us up. Joel spoke of ziplining possibilities, there they were. We marveled at what we knew would be above us, there it was, the speakers said *The world's largest high-definition screen*. We walked under the Fremont Street Experience and people flew over us on the SlotZilla Zip Lines, here was this place of wonder and curiosity, human excitement and fantasy. We passed one band on one stage then a half-block later another band on another stage... under and within street lights and crowds we took the four-casino crosswalk, passing street performers wearing sexual outfits, surrounded by and immersed in living surfaces.

Under the superficial there's something super, that's a human fact. We soaked it up, its energy traveled within us. When I looked at Joel under the lights I felt light. Bingo. The night was a tremendous success to me. The kind of night I think I should be having. For experience.

Basically, the downtown night gave my emotions a contact buzz. We returned to HoJo, we walked around the strip for a short while, then we embraced our tiredness, looking forward to the next day.

Then John ordered In-N-Out upon arrival, ahead of us was our new vacation day. Hell yeah.

Within this context everything was basically marvelous mostly. Vegas was an ocean of culture, dreams and trash. We bet on horse races at New York New York Casino, John paid for a Texas Hold Em tournament within the Excalibur Poker Room (I was the first to lose)... we sidewalked The Strip but felt most pure at night on Fremont... we played blackjack at the five-dollar tables within Golden Gate, our dealers had their names on their chokers, sweet and bad women, my favorite, and when they weren't dealing they were dancing on a platform between the gambling tables, which to me was slightly uncomfortable or awkward but whatever, it was meant to be fun, the pit bosses dressed like pimps, the expression is *Sex sells always has always will*, I like the style of sex, and here is where we felt most honest and relaxed while gambling in Vegas... also we discovered across from Las Vegas Blvd the Fremont East District, which was laid back and weird, two other favorite qualities, like John and Joel going down slides in the adult hours of Container Park, outside of which a metallic and robotic preying mantis shot fire over passing spectators...

...and only once, at Excalibur in the afternoon, an hour before poker and after John had reminded me, by coughing, that smoking is a nuisance, not necessarily because of that moment but after it I branched off from my friends to wander and wonder within the casino alone as if it were a Los Angeles sidewalk... a spell of my fears came over me and I asked the ground what I was going to say to these people, what the hell I was going to do with these people, who are so unlike me, as if it's not the same world we live in... and the ground told me that life was overall hopeless, impossible... and I thought of Luciana, she entered my thoughts and enters the story like mist from under the stage, and I remembered she'd mentioned the feeling of being overwhelmed by misery from the challenges of social interactions and having to be yourself... had we shared fights we ourselves created and could we have conquered them together... John, Joel and I then met up to eat before poker, Joel asked me if I was having a good time, I told him I was just restless like probably they were, although in retrospect they might not have been feeling restless... then I picked myself up from low feelings and back into shared smiles with old friends, which was both the most obvious option and the best one indeed...

...except then but well plus, sometimes at the end of my days my asshole mind takes a shit, and okay that night I crept out alone from the hotel to buy cigarettes at a normal price, from the Rebel gas station off the strip (the strip sells cigs for exorbitant prices), and then while taking a chain-smoking break I began to think of life outside love and myself in that place now... I wondered how I could do this, life, and if I could... I wondered with whom I could possibly continue to exist with in this world which feels like it could be perfect but never is... I missed her strength against the bleak... and which other person will have her strength I wondered... I thought about how I'm strong but with another person I can be stronger, so without another person I lose strength, yes... had I never been part of anyone's strength... and after my lonesome thoughts fumed into the night's sky I returned to HoJo, where we three old friends spoke again of classmates we missed and could remember, and with the beds pushed together we smiled and talked then slept until the next day, our last day.

The final Sunday night, after we returned again from Fremont, while in our hotel room I told my friends of Luciana. I hadn't been saving her story for sharing with them, but inside my mouth her wings took flight.

[Omitted Instagram context.]

I told them how the breakup had been at the beginning of this month, after the conclusion of two months together. The night of our breakup we hadn't talked resolution we'd talked perspective, and the gap between our perspectives, of emotion and logic, became great enough that she saw herself on another side. Had I helped her, I had. I'd first introduced a breakup to our breakup phone conversation. She'd asked me *Are you breaking up with me?* and I'd paused before I'd said *I can't respect a person who walks away*. Then she broke up with me. She could do what I couldn't, but I hadn't thought that needed done. The next day when I dreamed of love prevailing she clarified by text that we'd broken up.

For how long will she be a ghost in my thoughts, when I wished she weren't a ghost at all?

She'd been miraculously beyond-rare to me. Nah, yeah. Women. They're around. I'm a big fan in general. But there is too this world its fights these days and ways we bring ourselves through them. There are the specifics. The details. And all of hers I'd adored, from a strong philosophical perspective, which does indeed mean more than blind love, but still less than total picture, and but this is to speak of the past and not the present... I told my friends how at first it seemed safe, but recently it'd felt harder, that she was also my coworker. Working with her was similar to our relationship like this: we enjoy each other yet struggle at being with each other. I used to ask her why she didn't talk to me at work. She had told me she was working. Later she began talking to me at work. I found myself being the one just working. And what is rational and what is irrational in this blizzard of emotions?

Those philosophical blizzards I now and then walk myself within, no one's storms but my own.

I told my friends I didn't desire for her thoughts about me to be what guided my life, which perspective in fact inspired her to break up with me, but seemed tricky from my former and present eyes. I told my friends I couldn't imagine how she'll be in my life any longer, but I didn't want to push her out from my life forever.

My friends, after nods, and tender silence, they told me that because I kept mentioning how recently for some reason I've been way more attracted to non-white women, they'd been considering hiring me a black prostitute. Indeed I'd been thinking about getting a blowjob from a prostitute before this trip. But because I felt uncomfortable even when describing this prospect, I knew it wasn't a prospect for me. Also I clarified it wasn't necessarily any non-white who magnetized me. Told them I'm magnetized by rebel nerd outsiders. I described a non-white woman with glasses and a leather jacket on a street in London as a potential example. They told me they'd been investigating on the internet, saw some promising options. This trip had gone and will end without pot, without alcohol, without a hooker. I only smoked cigarettes kind of a lot, and caffeine was consumed in various ways by each of us. We didn't dress for Vegas we dressed natural and relaxed, like normal people having normal days... felt nice.

Then John rose as a cloud of butterflies, bringing out from his luggage two of my books, *Larry Angeles* and *My Autobiography Is My Manifesto*, asking me to sign their front pages. Which after I did I then apologized for what I'd written him not being too impressive, telling him I could have written his better maybe. Told him of another time I'd done a better job. What I wrote for *Larry Angeles* was I threw him minor shade for not having finished reading the book yet, and for *My Autobiography Is My Manifesto* I just reminded him that he's mentioned in the book because he means so much to me (which book also mentions how much he, and Joel, mean to me). My wish was I'd written on his title pages stronger words to reflect the strength this trip and he bringing my books had given me.

John said they were chill, great job.

After dropping John off at the airport and while traveling back to Barstow, where Joel and I had intersected Friday afternoon, he having driven from and returning to Napa Valley, on Monday morning Joel and I stopped in Baker. We passed Alien Fresh Jerky and the World's Tallest Thermometer. Then we ate at Burger King. Breakfast items. I wondered with him about the people who live here in this place which has nothing but these few businesses, out here in the desert around nothing, how do they live these people? We agreed the lady at the counter was a fabulous person, pondered how she was.

He dropped me back off at the Barstow Park & Ride. I drove my ninety-nine red Acura back to Los Angeles. Upon arriving in my apartment I found two fabulous mail items: high school graduation photos of my nieces Claire and Olivia, in an envelope addressed to The Godfather, and Sammy Dress clothes had arrived from Hong Kong (I'm Olivia's godfather and recently I'd been remembering Bill Cunningham's remark *Fashion is the armor to survive the reality of everyday life*).

While my roommate sat on his sheet-covered couch, typing on his computer, in front of a fan I ironed a floral-sleeve business shirt. I sweat. I took a shower. Then I put the shirt on and walked to work, briefly passing Luciana as she left from her shift while I arrived for mine. I got along with my coworkers, even during popular agreement that my shirt was nice but the sleeves resembled the carpet of a '70s hotel. Yasmin while nodding and shrugging said *It's a look.* Worse things have been said.

The next day back I worked alongside Luciana and cherished seeing her. She seemed to like seeing me. This day I wore a different shirt I forget which one. These were days which while they happened I wasn't thinking I must remember them. Vegas had felt warm and days had passed and being back at work I felt better.

What transpired? Instincts. Human nature. My susceptibilities.

At the start of her lunch and at the time of my break, Luciana rested across from me against the Customer Service counter.

I found her eyes.

I mimed cigarette smoking, fingers to my lips.

She nodded.

Outside on a wooden bus stop bench across from Maggiano's I gave us each a cigarette.

I mentioned buying this cigarette brand made me think of

her.

I reminded her that my no-show socks were because of her, which she already knew.

I was thinking out loud to this person about her lasting impact on my life.

I said *I thought of you in Vegas when...* then I grew quiet. I asked how she'd been.

Neither of us wanted to be where we had never wanted to be, neither of us wanted to return again to worries we knew, and to her that day I was worry embodied.

So, she mentioned this.

She told me she saw her sponsor who called her out for some *bullshit*. She said she shouldn't have been in a *relationship*. She said it was *the same thing as before*, as if I'm the same as another guy who's not me. She said she had begun to feel *worse*. She mentioned *isolationism*.

When she first told me of isolationism was after our breakup. At work she'd approached me and asked *Are you mad at me?* and I'd said *No* and she said *You look upset today* and I said *It's just a day* and she asked again if I were mad at her and I said no again and then I said *I don't... understand. What kind of friends are we?* then she shrugged and said *We saw The BFG* (after our breakup), so I said *I like the sound of this. We could eat somewhere...* (she had told me all she does with friends is eat and see movies), then she told me she doesn't see anyone now, she told me *It's called... isolation* and walked away as if the matter was settled. The next day I texted her, asking if she wanted to eat with me at Canter's a day later, since I had gift certificates. I heard from her the day we'd've eaten that instead she's going to see her sponsor.

What I said to her regarding the topic of isolationism having transpired from us, *You're exaggerating*.

There was her darkness and my sass. They're equally hard qualities but I think sass is harder.

I said *You missed two meetings one week?*

She replied *You're already becoming upset.*

I mentioned *I'm not upset, that was sass.*

I hadn't felt upset I'd felt natural. I certainly hadn't wanted to unleash an upset feeling into the moment. Nope, my goal hadn't been to go outside and get upset. In the background of my thoughts were the meetings she did go to. The fellowships she had. I'd known I'd never mean to her what her meetings did, her meetings and fellowships would continue... what of the people we saw together, places we went to together, were there ways for she and I to see places and people together again? The answer was outside my reach and getting further.

One can't always share one's emotions with another person, no.

She was the most analytical person I'd ever met. As everything else, analytics have their pros and cons.

She and I would often see and hear through our fears which our thoughts explored.

Still we knew there was more than fear.

One fear of mine wasn't being with her on the bench.

I liked being with her on the bench.

We knew our eyes were not the same.

I told her I was beginning to see from *her eyes*.

I could see our relationship was over.

I asked if she could see from *my eyes*.

She told me she had. *Yeah*.

She even nodded. Oh, damn.

Am I that easy, is this moment, or both?

Could she see that I'd never wish for us to evaporate like this?

I thought she could see my side but not see from it. I could forgive her because I had the same problem. Some of me was obvious: our breakup had unwound me, the instance of its occurrence had twisted me, and that little night which became so tragic inspired nothing but my guilt, motivating a thorough examination of my particular malfunctions as a person, and my misplaced emotions, which emotions I myself tend to celebrate.

These not feelings mentioned on the bench but my feelings on the bench. She knew only what I showed her, and what I'd mentioned in the eight-page poem about my personal disarray I'd written and which she'd read, so I showed nothing of myself on the bench. Our past remained nothing but incompleteness. I finished my cigarette and lit another one. I suggested we talk about movies instead (the cultural version of talking about the weather).

She said she'd seen *Ghostbusters* and wasn't impressed. I asked her if she wanted another cigarette. She said she didn't. She told me she wished *Ghostbusters* had more [name]. I said Paul Feig's talent perhaps wasn't writing but improv. She said she didn't blame anyone, but only wanted more [name]. I forget the name, hadn't seen the movie.

She said she was becoming less interested in entertainment movies. I said they suck.

We walked back to the bookstore having light conversation. I put my arm around her right shoulder for a short bit, since there she was, then I glided to her right side, switched back to her left, then she looked back at me and I said *Where am I?* We shared smiles.

Going up the escalator inside she told me this and that related to work.

Later I came down to the first floor, where she worked as Head Cashier, and when I passed her she said *Hey what up?* in a cheerful tone. I didn't know what to say back, I said nothing. Who was it that we were to be then? I still couldn't understand. This woman whom I've stopped texting, calling, or messaging, having done those things before, past when she stopped, at work she acts as if we're walking on clouds.

And aren't these the thoughts I'd begun to ponder and didn't want to ponder any longer? Yes.

But, so, I pondered what was happening again. Then I thought what I always think about her: I want to be around her when I can be around her.

Later I went again to the first floor, leaned against a shelf and asked her *What are you doing after work?* and she said *Nothing, going home* and I said *Do you want to hang after work?* and she said *Sure* and my feelings returned with me back up the escalator.

Then, when later I passed her leaving from the break room, she told me *Sorry, reversal on our plans... Nathan is closing cafe alone and I'm going to drive him home.* She turned away and I said *Hey* and she turned to me and I said *I tried*. She scoffed and walked out the door without looking back at me.

When I saw her during the store's closing meeting I thought of other things. Harry Potter was the hot topic because during my Las Vegas vacation *Cursed Child* had been released. So the meeting happened, happened, and when I felt the meeting could be ending I said *Can we drop Harry Potter?*, and the meeting ended and I clocked out and left without saying goodbye to anyone.

Returning home I didn't agree with myself for leaving without saying goodbye. I didn't like how I'd told her *I tried* as if she'd been put to a test and failed.

Texts having their emotional limitations, I called her and left a voicemail saying I wanted to break the tension which might appear as if between us. I mentioned calling for small talk. We were both hyper-aware of the line between intimacy and small talk. But I couldn't talk with her while talking to myself (ever). I felt this then. I made an embarrassing pause. I couldn't imagine having small talk into her voicemail so I didn't.

After I hung up I reflected.

Then after some few minutes I called her again. I waited through the rings, hoping to find her.

I left her a voicemail saying that trying for a second time is just like me.

That's mostly what I said.

This what she wanted to escape from.

Our romance over, she not someone I wanted to call Some

Whomever, whom was she becoming?

Further and Further Away.

And I didn't want to chase her, no. I wished to cherish but not to worship.

Reminder: outside one now is the next now.

Outside my social tragedies following this romantic failure was the rest of life and other romantic failures.

For his own reasons in his own story, Bruno at work was headed to Arizona to be another store's Merchandise Manager. Both Luciana and I Facebook confirmed we'd be attending Bruno's going away party at Shatto 39 Lanes.

Al would be at the going away party too. Where'd she come from? She came from life. We'd found each other in the bookstore. I Facebook messaged her about our mutual invitations I'd noticed, mentioning the situation was perfect for us since we couldn't bring drama to Bruno's going away party. She messaged back that she agreed and we would see what happened. I messaged her when I'd be there probably. She messaged me she'd be there when she was. Then I messaged her again right before the party, saying us at the party was no big deal, telling her that even we sharing these messages accomplished the intentions of the messages. So I went later than when I said I would and thought not of her but did I. Then after I'd been there and done this/that I sat next to a man from Ohio, his own story within him, the bookstore's Receiving Room Manager. And while I sat there Al arrived at Shatto 39 Lanes. She walked into a group near the bowling lane. I was back at a table. I told my manager of this being the one who got me my job. I motioned to her with my hands the question of whether she should walk to me or if I should walk to her. She motioned toward me. The manager suggested I meet her in the middle which I did. We met and stood in the hall behind others while our year-half tension shattered like ice, even when I sometimes spoke too quietly and she had to lean in to ask, *Sorry?*, needing me to repeat myself. She made nervous hand gestures. I did too behind my back. Within and outside our fears we shared human aspects... it took no effort for us to want to talk with each other that night. No part of me felt pressured to be there with her. In fact while wondering about pressure I glanced around the bowling alley and mentioned to Al that I didn't want to hog her from other people. She told me I wasn't. We talked, chatted, most of this catch up, which is always simple, sometimes fun, people laying their foundations which form buildings or don't. Most of the topics already over. We acted natural. I asked her if she'd gotten my email which referenced the ending of *Taxi Driver* (this email also saying Betsy was maybe nice since she'd gotten into the taxi but, anyway, our futures were like theirs now... over forever. This was around a year after our break up and a random email derived from thoughts of Al which *Taxi Driver* inspired within me. I relate to Travis Bickle in certain ways which depend on my life when I watch that movie). She said yes she got that email and she hadn't responded because what could she say. I asked her if I sounded complicated and confusing, *me??*, sassing myself, and because it's always easiest to sass yourself she laughed, and I asked her not to hold it against me, then behind a smile she told me she never would. A thing I know is you can't trust just a smile. We agreed that *Taxi Driver* is a great movie. She said she hadn't seen it recently. She told me she lived near me and looked for me sometimes when driving to work. She said she looks for me at the corner of Beverly and Fairfax especially. But she never sees me. I was like *What that's crazy,* since I walk around so often. She and I agreed this conversation was one step forward for us. I mentioned *Our futures are uncertain*. How good it felt to speak of a future during a wonderful moment and not a fit of worry or surrender. She mentioned we might pass by each other since we see the same types of movies. I mentioned a movie playing this weekend, invited her and her boyfriend, still she said that was like not happening but thanks. She said she'd maybe see me at AFI Fest. I said *Thinking of AFI Fest fucking traumatizes me*, then we talked about something else. We talked as friends. During our conversations Luciana left and half-swiveled toward me before turning to face the exit, waiting for a guy coworker, with whom she was leaving, he stopped to tell me goodbye, and that situation felt awkward but awkward is fine, fine, and I didn't feel bad because ice was on the floor. After Al and I shared various personal stories, including she telling me she wants to switch from her job position because she *don't want to work those nine-to-fives*, and she told me of recent depression, these things things we have in common, the fight, the spirit, then she went to chat with another friend, then I went outside to find the other smokers and then I returned to sit next to the manager, to whom I said *I'm going to treat this party like Seinfeld treated his show and split before things go downhill* as my goodbye intro, having already shared over Facebook that my party method is *arrive late, leave early*, then I walked to Al and asked her if she'd walk me out, she nodded and said to wait a moment, then I searched for Bruno to tell him goodbye, and while with Bruno she began to walk by, I said her name, we three shared brief conversation, I kissed Bruno on the cheek and said I'd miss him, she said *Wish I took a picture*, then she and I went outside and I apologized for being weird and she said this wasn't weird since she knows me and I said I was glad we could talk again I said I needed to tell her goodbye same as I needed to tell Bruno goodbye and I mentioned again that our futures were mysterious for certain reasons but they were futures so that's chill and as we had in the hall she said *Let's hug again* then I was back on the sidewalk then I was back in my car then I was back in my apartment then it was another day.

Not able to control my reality I retreated back inside the imaginary realities of books. Books tuck the outside world inside words, as our emotions tuck the world inside our heads. Everyone outside has their Interior Everything, and I'm a sucker for people's own words.

If only the world were a book and if only a book were the world. If only the world were an emotion.

If ifs and buts were candies and nuts we'd all have a Merry Christmas.

Beginning to read Alexandra Naughton's *American Mary* allowed me to perceive and relate with exploration from an interior/exterior world into a word-substance existence. Then, owing to a chance encounter at work, one day I decided I should obviously read Rainer Maria Rilke's *Letters to a Young Poet*, so I finally did, while writing a goodbye letter to a coworker, Valerie, who worked in the cafe. She was an illustrator headed to CalArts next week. In my goodbye letter I wrote that I cherish her art but that's not what I cherish most about her. I called her a good person in an eternal sense, eternity on my mind from Rilke, along with my general fondness for this coworker.

I wrote that I think people need her.

People who are good to people are good people.

I try my best and fuck up, that's my style.

Early hellos and early goodbyes were recurring social blunders of mine.

I wrote her her goodbye letter before she left so I didn't have to keep asking her when she'd leave. I thumb-tacked the note onto the cafe's bulletin board.

The next time I saw Valerie she was thankful. She was excited to see me. She was working in the cafe. I stood before her cash register and I sensed that the substance of the letter wasn't immediately compatible with our reality.

I hadn't felt bummed but I'd felt its tinge. The letter didn't pour out of me then, nah. I smiled. She smiled. I asked for a venti chocolate milk and a blueberry scone.

I mentioned Rainer Maria Rilke. She mentioned she might put my letter up in her college room. Once, she drew a portrait of me for myself. I have it saved it my room. When I saw her after she made it she told me she liked it enough that she might post a photo of it on her site, which she didn't. Will my letter hang in her room?

There are words and truth, wishes and reality. How many actions become words and how many words become action, I forget.

In the moment in the now it's simply a matter of looking at the other person. But what of the person from before and the person from after... is the topic of worry another person's past or future? And why worry?

Also I read *Every Time We Meet at the Dairy Queen, Your Whole Fucking Face Explodes* by Carlton Mellick III. Because of Mellick, who helped establish it, I discovered the literary enterprise of bizarro fiction, which is the expulsion of emotions into slipstream genre forms, by contemporary authors with fantasy and sci-fi interests. The overlap between what's called objective and what's called human. What's for adults and what's for kids. Discovering bizarro fiction excited me, I ordered more of its books with immense curiosity regarding future reading pleasures potentially obtainable from *A God of Hungry Walls* and *The Night's Neon Fangs*. [Omitted section about more books in more shopping carts.]

I had the money to order books from having canceled a recent re-order I'd made at Sammy Dress. Learning the difference between Asian and American clothing sizes was most problematic for me when I ordered a jacket and suit coat. I thought I was supposed to order larger sizes but when they arrived they were simply too large. This had been money given to me by my sister in July for my birthday in February, so I'd liked the jacket and coat and went to a tailor, my first time at a tailor, who measured me, and we agreed it'd be more cost efficient for me to re-order these cheap nice clothes than for her to fix them, and paying for return postage didn't appeal to me, so I just did the re-order but what happened was Sammy Dress was unable to ship within their estimated time, so instead of store credit I asked for a refund, and in these later days I felt more inclined to spend my money on books.

Books are the armor to survive the reality of everyday life. Books are purchased to be read, as clothes to be worn. Although some books I buy without reading, guilty. Before finishing *American Mary*, which had been interrupted by *Letters to a Young Poet*, I read Carolyn Zaikowski's *In a Dream, I Dance By Myself, and I Collapse*. This book pulled me in. Its conceptual versatility. Its adventurous narrative patterns and its human center. The fear of emotions I found relatable. The outrageousness of everything. I had the good kind of read as I enjoyed it to its final page.

Also, when I was feeling some emotions I was vibing some music. Always. Drama Duo's "Forever's Gone" I considered an electronic power song for my soul. *You see / What you want to see* Via Rosa sings. I thought about this song in relation to Luciana. I thought about her thinking about this song in relation to me. I thought about us seeing the same world with different eyes. I put the song in my playlist of current favorite songs, along with "Glowed Up" and "Got 'Til It's Gone". I appreciate songs about getting through the fight. I believe the fight exists and I believe strength is needed. I search for these qualities within art, people, and elsewhere, everywhere, always.

I've learned the most about being a person through art. This has been helpful since, the universe not having a human condition, being a person is its own art form. People as art, people as reality, my ultimate belief the life I see and live, this gets tricky, tricky, for example sometimes a person in front of me isn't being who they really are. There's a tremendous difference between a bad person and the art of crankiness. Given the moment, I may not be able to spot the difference! There are the arts of tiredness hunger and fear. There are the arts of sickness and the human body. And what of giddiness? Hallelujah. Sometimes one knows the art without knowing the person, sometimes one knows the person without knowing their art, sometimes one never knows the person and there was no art. Me, around others I often attempt to enter inside eyes not mine, and there in their eyes I can lose myself, I can lose the other person too, and during my stronger moments I remember what I'm looking for is already there. For example I'm already here, here in this text. And the truest part of this text, this having been written by me already, all that's real and holy about these words comes now from the reader, who can't be alone here with me. I can't be alone here with you. Here we are together. Always: there is more than one's worries in this world, for example other people's worries. And movies. I saw with a coworker, who shared a pass with me, a Maurice Pialat double at the Billy Wilder Theater. The vibrancy of *Loulou* I found glorious, infectious. *Under the Suns of Satan* was a dark, downer of a movie. Its first ten minute were my favorite, when the priest, Gérard Depardiue, talked about how he has terrible memory and other intellectual difficulties, so he feels fucked. I found that feeling relatable. But then the entire movie portrayed this. That was heavy. Life is heavy, agreed. Life can be too heavy, so let art be light, in order to perhaps inspire more lightness in life. I thought *Loulou* had both the unbearable and the light, both movies had their sense of being, but me I'd rather be a person living *Loulou* than a person living *Under the Suns of Satan*. My coworker agreed. Then shortly later, after a couple days, this coworker shared another movie pass and we saw *Little Men* at Laemmle's Royal Theatre. What was funny to me was in *Little Men* two boys gave their parents the silent treatment. The movie had originally been titled *The Silent Treatment*. Life in art in life. New York was often better than Los Angeles at putting life into movies, I thought. Except I didn't like *Little Men* very much, and my coworker liked it very much. I thought its existential montages were hash, underage kids in a club scene was an admirable quality that didn't feel like a discovery, I thought, though my coworker maintained the course that *Little Men* was lovely, said *It'll be remembered after we're gone*, which was an intense thing to say (I'd asked him to repeat it). We had agreed about the scene with the frustrated teen crying while attempting in vain to reach compromise with his parents, concerning the nature of caring about other people, great scene, and we continued to get along through the night, though still the night's rewards diminished while he found treasures within the movie and I found frustrations. Plus I was restless, and after eating ice cream outside Milk he brought me home. We didn't kiss goodbye on the cheeks as we had other times. I wouldn't see him again for a couple of days, until I saw him at work and we got along fine, but we didn't jump back into making future plans.

Really, I barely interact with anyone and when I do I think maybe it could matter but nothing matters because of the need to matter, things only matter when they do, I should think about something else, like my reality, that'd be a healthy choice.

Though still, a person can live with worries. Live.

On occasion sometimes I wondered how much thought I should put into me with my coworkers. People whom I knew because we were often in the same building together, pondering what other reason we were together for.

Thinking of people is far, far different from being with them. When I was alone in my apartment and worrying over how my coworkers felt about me I always thought this: *really?* The world has over seven billion people and I could think about something a coworker said to me as if those words had the weight of everything. I thought too about the things I said to my coworkers, friends and family, and I wondered and worried about the weight of words. There it was: the heaviness of life. Since life makes itself unbearable, in my opinion, it's life's lightness I must search for and find. Some of my coworkers and friends and family could sometimes be such wonderful people! May I remember that when they were not. And, when there is fortune in my fate, may they remember the same for me.

I tried to hatch defensive schemes sometimes. For example I tried not to carry the thoughts of my coworkers home with me. My coworkers were how I saw them at work. *I'll see you when I see you.* My feelings for them didn't need to reach beyond my eyes. I could remember the big picture and things would be fine. The internet, e.g. Facebook and Instagram, same there, things would be fine if I didn't say they weren't. I orchestrated these schemes to avoid problems wondering who cares about me and who doesn't. I longed to avoid nervousness related to not knowing who I know about. I was a paranoiac.

But, also a romantic. People: wonderful. All of them. Most of them. Some of them sometimes always.

I couldn't believe there were seven billion people in the

world and I knew, what, like about two hundred of them. Friends with about six of 'em. There were so many more people than the people I knew. I knew the people I knew. California wasn't Ohio or was it? Is that confusing no that's not confusing California wasn't Ohio so why had I felt like it was... was the bookstore like high school? Within all these people it was still the few who came to feel like family. Isn't that always the case...

Too, there's the place and the place within the person. These thoughts around me and within me, although I wish only one thought happened at once, my days happened how they did, and later one night I made it through a work shift without having a conversation with Luciana. She wasn't my first thought in my mornings any longer. Sometimes I forgot of her. Sometimes I thought of her with terror.

I chose not to worry about her future mind shifts nor my own. When she talked to me I talked back. But I looked not for her these days. In fact, one day while she was coming down the escalator onto the first floor where I was, I ducked inside a back room. Had she seen me I didn't know, didn't wonder. She having seen my worst she feared the worst when she saw me. That was terrifying. Behind me were the days when I dreamed of making her days wonderful. Still, the issue was I didn't want her to be Some Whomever. Who had I wanted her to be? Wonderful each day however she could be... though I couldn't see myself within her days.

I didn't know these were our final-final days, and our last day would be microcosmic of our entire relationship. I didn't know our future would explode I never did. I didn't dream of fucking explosions.

So Luciana was at work and there I was too and none of this mattered. Oh I liked her smiles and I think she liked mine but we'd never understood what made the other person smile. While she was there we were a silent movie of deadpan emotions.

Trying not to think about each coworker of mine as a worry, yet finding some worrisome from their methods and my own, one day I went down the escalator. There I went, was going. Then I turned around and there she was. Aside a coworker I couldn't quite figure out. That was a pickle. I turned my head back around. I stood half-akimbo, a bent wrist against my hip, in my orange patterned collared shirt. I looked like an idiot. I thought I heard Luciana say, *This is what I would expect*, I had heard the coworker laugh, and there was another escalator, then while leaving the building I saw Luciana hug another coworker who was a friend and I thought of those hugs and how they arrive, then she branched toward the exit, me behind her and the first coworker, then they split paths and I saw Luciana walk under the sun on her own path away from me again, not saying anything, and while passing the coworker I reflected on this moment, which didn't feel right to me. I didn't like the feeling of that situation in pretty much every way. It was rife with petty dramas. I went to Chipotle to order my food, but the line was long, so instead I began as if I'd already begun to head toward the eighth floor of the parking garage, where I thought Luciana might be taking a smoke break. There in the open, outside of other people's eyes, was where I wanted to see her and talk with her again. Life wasn't as difficult as it felt difficult to be around her, I knew. Life was better and she was better than life and I walked over the eighth floor under the sun but I didn't find her. Then I headed back inside to work. Well, first I washed my hands in the bathroom, where I saw another coworker. I'd recently wondered about this coworker and me. Wondered whether he liked me or didn't. Trying not to think about how other people may or may not like me, and wanting to think of others but desiring neither attention nor worry, I was trying to be *Whatever* about this, and all there was was right then, but so right then I asked him in the bathroom, *Hey, is there tension between us?* He said to me, bit shocked, *No, why would there be?* Oh good. I told him, *Couldn't figure out why either. Glad I asked.* He said *I'm feeling emotional.* I said *I was feeling emotional, that's why I asked.* He said *Okay.* Then while we were leaving he asked, *Did you hear someone got fired* and no I hadn't heard that. I wondered about it, we went into the office for info, couldn't ask then, so we went back to work and time went on. When I heard it was Luciana my face dropped, I said *I have to make a call,* I dashed across the third floor onto a balcony chair, left her a voicemail, then I returned to work, felt astonished and miserable. Already for me there was a palpable contrast between she being there and she being gone. How would I be reminded of how strong she is, I wondered, and I knew that though this day felt terrible to me, this day felt worse for her, and unrelated to me, so on my break I called and left her another voicemail, I told her *Reminder: you have a wonderful smile. You have a wonderful laugh. You're a wonderful person.* I told her about my eighth floor search for her. I told her I wished we'd had our goodbyes. I told her that not only couldn't I believe this happened, I couldn't believe it happened like this. Then I went back inside and she texted me a thank you. I had told her on my second voicemail that that was my last phone call to her, but after her text I texted that I'd call her when I got off work. I wanted to be there for her, and I was in denial about not being able to be there for her. When would I see her again I wondered, which wonder I left on a voicemail when I called her that night, and we had not made plans, she had told me she was going to a meeting, she'd texted *Goodbye,* but so after the voicemail I reflected on what I'd said in my voicemail and how I'd said it, and I reflected on my nows which would no longer include her, and I remembered again that the hardest part of her day hadn't been related to me at all, this day had been a smack from life, I felt bad but she had it worse, and the next day I called again, I mentioned or didn't mention that it was like the last time I did this, mentioned or didn't mention that this is me, I had tried to call her again yes, and it was the same song but with different lyrics, I reminded her she's strong then I hung up from talking to myself, wanting to talk with her, she was *poof* gone, like that, gone, and then the next day I sent her a text which I described as a final letter, in which I told her that her best days are ahead of her because her best days are inside of her, I promised her that, believing it to be true, believing her to be wonderful, just a killer person overall, and now so far away from me that I'd need the Thirty Meter Telescope to see her.

Like that. Which when mentioned to her she seemed not to mind. I cut off from her on the internet, which also sounds like me, because life can feel so black and white to me when my heart is cut in half, and the grey area gets tough for me, especially when the black tends to be my area, while another may come into the white where they always belonged.

She seemed not to concern herself about anything related to us. All people, when they can, recognize emotional nonsense as such. She went away from me with such resolve. Such certainty. Me, being the one walked away from, yes, I had the feelings she left behind. She reminded me that my emotions are not reality, though I shift not by knowing but by feeling. I knew our relationship had ended. Then I felt it. And I felt what was beyond it, which felt to me like nothing.

I had told her and it's true, I don't stop caring about a person. I had told her I loved her when I told her goodbye, giving the reason of a midwestern tradition, which my mother taught me, that *When saying goodnight to a person you should tell them you love them, because you might not see them the next day.*

Some pasts are not futures.

Some days are the last.

I'm an eternal romantic and anyway all futures whatever they become inevitably become a new past anyway. This excites me: my future tense becoming my new past. I look forward to the past in front of me. My past behind me there it went. This is how I wiggle within eternity.

After I'd already crossed the proper and acceptable boundaries for conversation with Luciana, I did what I always do, instead of getting trapped in my misery I wrote it out of me. This can be called catharsis but I'd like to call it exorcism. This is historical nonfiction but is it... nonfiction is reality and reality is more than words. What means more to me: my life or my words? My life! I search for life within reality, and when I can't find it I search within words and love, which are both largely acts of invention, and, mentioning: love is in fact my favorite place where my imagination takes me, may I one day find myself there with another person. For now there's but these words. And I knew I had to write this the same I had known I wanted to be with Luciana. I follow my emotions, always. I'd told her back when that I'd write a poetry book about loving her! Back then. The pages I write can't be written into her life, which life I no longer imagine myself in. In terms of what that feels like, the reader can already have known that her eyes meant more to me than these words. My clock was inside her eyes while I was with her. Then that's true so okay what will be true next I wonder while wondering whether anything can be true. But here are my words, okay, tricky. Am I consumed by my life as it is or consumed by my life as it is in my mind...

Then it was Valerie's final day at work.

Again: my early goodbye to her had been early.

Me: always me.

I'd even since the letter conversation seen her another basic time I'm omitting.

Her final day she came over to the Customer Service area. I was helping a customer. She said goodbye to Maggie and Amanda, then I was able to see her for a second, there was a short hug and *I'll miss you.* Two coworkers were behind her with their human faces. Everyone was ready for the goodbye and I had already done the goodbye. There's what we thought this moment might be and what it was. The letter wasn't in this moment, no. My words were not my life, and what was my life I wondered. Will Valerie remember the letter and what did it matter... I listened again to the customer describe the book she needed help finding... will Valerie remember me? Valerie and the coworkers left. Will I remember Valerie? Did it matter, it did it does, but what matters more is tomorrow.

Here is a thing I know: life is both inside each second and bigger than each second.

Here is a thing I believe: life is inside each person and bigger than each person.

[First ending...]

So by the end of writing this I'm fully immersed. This: my life translated into words. It's common for a writer to close off the outside world for page immersion.

On a Saturday night, past midnight, so actually Sunday, I go to CVS. I had gone to Shell but they were closed, so, considering this a writing break, I took the longer walk to CVS. I just completed this short's first full draft.

Then while leaving CVS I hear my name being called. I turn around, see two people. I can't recognize them. I hear my name again and stand still until I notice they're two coworkers. I walk to my coworkers and they walk to me. This an accident of time and opportunity. Fate rattles. My coworkers tell me they've just gotten off work. I ask what time it is. *Oh.*

I'm holding a half-eaten ice cream sandwich in one hand, an unopened chocolate milk in the other. I listen to news regarding my coworkers' days. They're excited. I'm startled. Everyone smiles, acts natural. After they each tell me a story, since my own story would be me alone at home writing, I don't mention my story, I ask them how they're getting home. They tell me. I wonder: what can I say to these people, I want to tell them everything and I can't think of anything to tell them. We say goodbye. I turn and within the darkness of the evening I walk over the city sidewalks which exist outside the page.

Then I return to my apartment and enter inside pages again. In *The Sorrows of Young Werther* I underline *Being lost to ourselves, we lose everything.* While walking in my room I notice, behind my blue curtains, that my windows are closed. I open my windows. I hear *whooshes* from the city. Then I think: the past is in the present but the present isn't in the past.

Is there an epilogue.

There is.

Why.

Because of life, which I don't write.

Returning home from Karl and Megan's, some time after I started writing this, walking across Melrose on a Thursday afternoon I notice Luciana walking too. We're both smoking cigarettes. I think of what could happen if we crossed paths and, as I can't imagine what our sidewalk conversation would give either of us but moments from which we desire to be released, we both wanting to feel released, before we intersect I turn up a sidewalk instead. Then I dash into an alley, and I don't look back until I'm to when and where if I had seen her I would've walked toward her, yes I bet so, for the spirit, always, but as she was not there I continue to miss her as I continue to walk.

I don't turn around again until later when that would've been way, way ridiculous, if I had turned around and there Luciana was. She lingers in my daydreams. I know she'll never be there when I turn around. I wonder what her thoughts of me had been, had she seen me, and I think again about what matters and doesn't matter. I think my sunglasses had been crooked and did it matter.

Now I have the fan on, my bedroom curtains are open, and I'm in blue boxers with white polkadots. Wiggling my feet and wondering if I'm sweating too much, if I'm currently smelly. I should take a shower and after I've done that I'll have done that.

Has it been easier since Luciana left that I haven't seen her at work? Seeing her today was nothing but a tiny miracle, but some miracles do feel like disasters. I was glad to see her walking. I wish for the world to be treating her with kindness at least.

And there's what's written and what's said and what's real. Today I'm like this and tomorrow I could feel better or worse, it depends, because after the final line comes the next day and I don't already know the next day. I don't already know my own life story. I know you know what animal I am when I say I wish today wasn't today. But, today is today, and I know this: one life. Patience. In the end there's nothing but my days until I die. Now I'll return my words to the beginning; we're only my thoughts now. In the end I'm the same as I was in the beginning. I'm me during all my moments, every day, still me. I'm actually in the living room when I write the final line. Fan on, windows up. I need to shower.

NeuroPark

Recently Razmik had been having difficulties being a person, which was at the back of his mind while he was eager to hear Leonard's story, and see Yasmin again, so he was ultra-excited when for these very reasons he teleported from Kolkata at ten-thirty on a Saturday morning into Los Angeles at nine o'clock on a Friday evening.

Not time travel but basic globular teleportation, from downtown Kolkata to downtown Los Angeles (Bunker Hill, which Leonard had suggested for its *artsiness*).

That night Razmik gazed onto a Los Angeles street and wondered if he had arrived on a better side.

He wasn't sure, but didn't think he had. He considered: Kolkata, a ball of energy; Los Angeles, a sad casino filled by ghosts.

Razmik shook his legs as he walked across the street toward the tasteful bar Paraíso. This where people go who don't worry about small things like the cost of drinks. Paraíso makes Leonard feel comfortable. Razmik will feel repulsed by its opulence but delighted by its ornamentation.

His eyes open upon his life, this city, and he felt as if there was too a whole city inside him, Razmik, being an adult, having learned his lessons, before entering Paraíso he stood and let the breeze kiss his body. He closed his eyes, exhaled, shaped his hands into fists.

He stood there reminding himself that he didn't know what the night would be. He reminded himself to expect nothing. He wanted not to invite his sadness into this night.

He exhaled again, blowing softly through his lips.

What can be known is true: the reader is alive, the people in this story are alive and the writer is alive now too, same planet, eleven and a half billion of us. This was December twenty-second of last year, which was the numerically palindromic year of twenty-one twelve for all of us. This story from this time and planet we share, what *needs* mentioned to give life its flight? What *needs* to be told, regarding practical and philosophical logistics? Everyone knows anything. That's literary existentialism. That's emotional psychology. That's the tyranny of choices upon the writer, who already worries his needs might not match the reader's. The writer worries. The writer is human. This story is about humans. The writer considers a human facts in flesh, a story flesh in words, and being a story is the same as being a human: formal shared fundamentals and small differences which end up mattering, good luck.

The writer refuses to get tangled in worries, which perseverance the writer says allows one to finish a story, and one may live as one writes, not by worries but by solutions, and anyway the end of this story already happened, its history is being converted from reality into words... point is, outside this story is a ceaseless world for everyone but, for the sake of this story, this world is only on this page. As a writer I have some pressure regarding truth (though pressure is never quite helpful to mention, my bad, but also too truth often feels more impossible than it should). Let it be hoped that readers can see these pages upon the public reality of this planet. And, remember: everyone will be fine by the end, if not simply since the end.

First things first: backstory. Razmik had heard about Leonard's NeuroPark from a mutual friend. The friend had given Razmik fuzzy descriptions of a Secret and Radical and

Progressive technology Within the Frontiers of Electronic Phenomenology. It had vaguely sounded as if Leonard somehow had access to fresh materials of the future. The friend wasn't certain where Leonard obtained this NeuroPark since, back then, before it became public a month ago, no one was chatting about NeuroPark. The friend had said *secret* eleven times. Razmik had thought: *What a kick.*

The friend had said that Leonard when he tells of NeuroPark he stipulates that it's his secret to share. The friend said he couldn't say much... later he said it *makes virtual reality feel like the stone age.*

Leonard had himself a magical secret, and Razmik is a fan of secrets, magic, and Leonard.

NeuroPark and Leonard grew like mold in his mind's cellar. Back when he heard about this, six months ago, he began hatching plans for seeing Leonard.

After much pondering he arrived at the bright idea of speaking to Leonard like a human being. He asked him: *What up, how you doing?*

A month later Razmik considered Leonard's non-response non-human. But it's common for Razmik when he begins an endeavor to hit a wall, and he learns only by his mistakes. Then he heard from someone else about NeuroPark. Razmik thought: *hearing about one secret two times bothers me.* He hadn't wanted to embarrass himself, so he contacted Leonard just one last time, three months ago, using a serious tone and a solemn approach straight to the matter of desiring to see Leonard.

He told him: *It feels necessary to see you now.*

[What is *it* and is *it* real?]

Again there wasn't a reply.

Upon reflection Razmik considered his first letter too flaccid, his second letter too desperate.

He feared plans he built with his feet of clay.

Then he tried not to think about this. He said to himself: *Not so bad.* He didn't want to call this bad.

He'd been rejecting negative wish fulfillment. Instead of dwelling on his tricky Leonard quandary, Razmik reviewed some of his other problems related to being a person.

Many of Razmik's current problems scurried in shadows beneath his personal fears. He called his current life a melodrama starring bugs in his soul.

Also, lately he'd been thinking his life might not be as bad as his worries, as it turns out each of his worries hasn't killed him yet.

He had also been willing to believe his life is simply he experiencing holographic virtual reality in hell.

Then he worried about how much worrying he was doing, all-the-time saying: *I wish my life wasn't like this, or this, or this, or this.* Over and over again he worried about his own life, about himself, and he worried he worried about himself often enough that his worries approach narcissistic properties.

That was pissing him off.

He was pissing himself off, which he tried to stop, or not care about, and he tried to point his emotions to a place where he thought they should be, but he couldn't even name such a place. He was trapped in himself and assessing disproportionate figures he gathered from his life and his worries.

Razmik wore around his personality dread as a robe, while Leonard wore dread as socks.

Leonard had Razmik's worries only on his foulest days. He rushed to his psychologist after and during such predicaments, fumigating his problem, which rarely turned out to come from the thing that bothered him, and then he returned to yoga and meditation within his skyscraper penthouse where he lived single but not alone. He lived with his mother, whom he adored. Always he escaped from the edges of his worries toward the center of his actions as fast as he could, diving into business affairs, draping his concerns, masking his personhood, living and loving while happening.

Before tonight Razmik and Leonard had met just twice, both times owing to another person. But Razmik believed the second time had a feeling of significance. It was a night of genuine male bonding. A rare commodity. They each, Razmik and Leonard, had divulged personal details saved for special times with certain people. It was pure chance, and wine, and Razmik first sharing some private dramatic story, which allowed Razmik to hear Leonard tell him, looking into his eyes, that his father never loved him, and his father was an emotionally abusive Marine veteran. Leonard told Razmik his personal success in life was unrelated to his father's existence. He said: *But here I am, talking about that asshole now.* He said: *That's because I'm drunk friendly, and you're good people.* He said: *Not only do I not usually talk about my father, but I rarely think about him, since thinking about him can trap my thoughts.* He said: *My life has been me hammering against the walls he tried to build in me.*

Razmik asked: *Is your father still alive?*

Leonard said: *Yes, and he's nice now.*

A pause hung in the room.

Razmik said: *Change doesn't mean better…*

Leonard nodded, threw back his glass of wine. Then he said: *He can't change how he already treated me and my mother.*

Razmik lived of the world and Leonard lived through it.

This, this is what happens: Razmik, pondering, stuck himself on the topic of only himself…. compared to Leonard, who committed actions from his ponderations.

Yet that night they each spotted the fight within the other person.

Razmik reminisced upon his great night with Leonard, avoiding thoughts concerning his recent social disasters. He maintained fondness in his memory, but he wondered about ultimate values. He wondered: *Did my stock numbers soar with Leonard or did they?*

NeuroPark, that fucking secret…

Razmik thought: *Fuck.*

The solution came on its own accord, which is typical for life problems.

A week prior to the night of this story, five months ago, Yasmin had contacted Razmik, wishing him a happy December, mentioning the coming year and its fresh curiosities, telling Razmik this and that, saying she and Max are fine, and saying Razmik should hear the story of their friend Leonard's goodie. She called his story a *firecracker*. Was this pure chance or purely cosmic? Pure story, but who was the writer that day in their lives? Razmik told her he was glad she was well, said he'd heard about NeuroPark, and he needed to hear everything about it. She said she related to his need, and he should come visit them in Los Angeles. He said he should. Pacing his room before he left for his visit some days later, Razmik wondered what the story would be like when he heard it, and how he'd feel after hearing it.

Max and Leonard have had years of sturdy friendship, Max being how Razmik first met Leonard, and it was through Max that Yasmin got to know Leonard better. Max and Razmik have met several times. Max is an okay guy, Razmik thinks. He most appreciates his friendship with Yasmin, which friendship she appreciates too. Their friendship formed years back when Razmik grew as a person around other people in Los Angeles growing the same. Razmik lived in Los Angeles as a young adult until he'd felt he'd had enough, then he left, as others of his friends had, and other friends had stayed in Los Angeles. Change happened and didn't. Some people remained friends and some people didn't.

Years passed regardless.

Razmik and Yasmin remained friends. The reason? The same reason as always: because they did, and they will until they don't.

The night of this story, inside Paraíso, Razmik found a table that appeared to him as a lighthouse within his recent dark sea voyage:

Razmik, who is Razmik, found Leonard, who is Leonard, sitting across from Max, who is mostly unrelated to the story.

When approaching Razmik questioned whether to hug them or shake their hands.

Leonard smiled without moving while Razmik sat down, awkward.

Max glanced across his shoulder toward the bathroom, then he faced Razmik while nodding, then he winked before saying: *Bathroom*, which Razmik knew meant Yasmin was there.

Razmik would have preferred this situation if Yasmin was already there with them. Razmik, with others now but lost in his own thoughts still, while his eyes landscaped Paraíso Leonard said to him: *Well we meet again*. Razmik turned to Leonard and said: *Agree*, he smiled, felt confused, then Leonard smiled and while rubbing Razmik's arm he said: *Hey buddy*.

Razmik remembered he thinks Leonard is a solid guy. He smiled. They smiled. Success.

Razmik turned to Max and said: *I'm seeing you*.

Max nodded, bit his lip.

Razmik said: *Feels good*.

Max unbit his lip, said: *Feels good*. Then a second later he started biting his lip again. Max felt uncomfortable that day for reasons not part of this story. He shook his head, picked up his martini, took a long sip. He was in his own head, in his own story.

Razmik stared at the rainforest again. He wished there was cheap food and drinks but he felt alright. While Razmik stared Leonard noticed Razmik had the weary face of an anxious person. Leonard barely knew Razmik. In his head Razmik was a composite from limited contact. Leonard thought Razmik for sure had too much anxiety.

Razmik, feeling himself being looked at, he turned his face toward Leonard, whose eyes were moving toward Razmik's tapping foot. Then Razmik noticed Max noticing something, and after he looked over so did Leonard.

Yasmin danced while she walked toward the table. She was the one who would break this discomfort and bring positive energy to the table. She had plutonic positivity. Her sweetness was radioactive.

Razmik stood and hugged her when she arrived. She squealed. She said: *Thu-rilled to see you.* She scooted next to Max on the couch near the table.

It brings a terrific feeling to a person, seeing an old friend in a familiar place. Razmik wasn't familiar with this bar, no, but he felt as if he was because he knew this city and he knew these people.

He was as comfortable as he could get he wasn't fully comfortable. He wished everyone wasn't wearing such expensive clothes. He looked at himself and tried not to think about his clothes. He wondered who was thinking about his clothes. He'd dressed without worrying what people might think about his clothes, and he regretted his earlier decision. He remembered: *Ignoring a worry at its foundation can cause the worry to grow as a building within you.*

He thought: *If I could rewind my day I'd start by dressing better.*

But he couldn't rewind.

Razmik looked across the table at Yasmin, who took a sip from her martini, then while holding Max's hand with her other hand she held out her martini to Razmik and said: *Take a sip!* He said: *No thanks.* She remembered he doesn't drink and smiled, took another sip of her martini. She fell and rested against Max's body.

Max, unfazed by Yasmin against him, he picked up his martini and took a long sip. While holding the martini glass in his hand he said to Razmik: *You should order a water or something.*

Now the background is the foreground and the context is in the people, the people are in the story. Razmik hadn't thought about water and he didn't want to. He didn't feel he needed to hold a glass to make Max feel comfortable. He didn't order water. Max took another long sip from his martini, finishing it.

It was then that music in the room grew quieter, the overhead lights turned off, and only the tables and waiter trays glowed with light. The holographic birds of paradise began to dance in front of video wall rainforests, mist floated from beneath chairs, and Razmik didn't blink his eyes.

The birds of paradise performed their mating dances, and Razmik let them impregnate his emotions with mellow children.

This lasted for several wonderful minutes, during which time most people in attendance uploaded images from their video-contacts onto their Thoughts for others to see. Or they stored images in their memory banks. Though it was a wildly popular and widely shared feature in Paraíso: the birds of paradise dancing within the long-gone rainforest. Few have seen it without saving a photo or memory.

During this time, Yasmin told the funniest joke Razmik had heard all year. He slapped his knee. Everyone involved themselves in a laughing intermission. Then Leonard told a story about buying a hoverbike from the black market, and it breaking on him after a month.

Then lights returned, and music from a soft guitar came into the room as Leonard said: *It was so annoying...* Then he began to smile, for a beautiful singing voice floated through the room.

Leonard mad vibed with this song that was a sad story of personal strength. The singer's sadness was in her words and her strength was in her voice. Her soul was in her voice, Leonard felt.

Yasmin, who seemed not to be listening to the song, while staring at Leonard's slanted head she said: *Razmik, my friend -- please define your life such that you define yourself, if your life defines you but, if it doesn't, please tell me something else.*

Razmik paused while he stared at his hands, at her eyes, at his hands, then he told her: *It feels good to see you.* Yasmin, nestled into Max, nodded. Max stared into the room at an obscure object, his vision unfocused, his thoughts trapped in his head.

Yasmin, unable to suction out a story from Razmik, but excited to see him and be merry with friends, she thought Razmik looked anxious so she tried to think what Razmik was outside of anxiety, and she told Razmik and Leonard a story of she and Max going to a pool on -- she pointed to where it was in geographic relation to Paraíso -- the roof of this downtown skyscraper. She said: *There we kicked our feet in water... Los Angeles stretched outside below us* [waves hand]... *we, us, feeling... as big as the city* [volcanic hand gestures]... *that's how we felt!*

She placed her hands on her lap, which for Leonard and Razmik was like seeing a bird place her legs upon the ground.

Wind was in her eyes they noticed.

Yasmin thought for a moment about how else she could describe this. Her hands soared again as she said: *I felt reminded, looking at the city, next to this dreamboat* [motioned to Max]... *reminded of my capabilities... as a human... humans are built to hold a city within them, I sometimes try to remember... sometimes, sometimes experiencing interior fantasies...* [she rubbed against Max's body, he squeezed her with his arm]... *for example while swimming in a rooftop pool at night, with the city quiet but for the sounds of him next to me....*Everyone smiled while Yasmin added: *Max is a pool in my heart hotel which I sit next to while reading from myself.* She placed her hands on her lap again. In her hands were the room's feelings. There was a silent beat. Then Leonard said: *Did you...* But Yasmin suddenly had more to say, so she cut in: *Like, our interior selves are the same as land, and we should build cities in ourselves... right?*

Everyone continued smiling as Yasmin punctuated her story's theme: *Our personal emotions begin as a country that can become a city. Or stay a country...*

She paused, reflected: *Everything felt so clear that night...*

Razmik knew well of people whose dreams expand in their minds while withering in their lives and stories. His worldview then was from Kolkata, where he lived alone-alone. During much of his private time he either wrote for nobody since nobody reads him or he read other writers, and to Yasmin, with whom he shares many interests, he mentioned: *Italo Calvino... writer, Italian, 20th century... postmodernism... his short story collection... Cosmicomics... if you've read it you know what I mean, if you haven't read it I recommend 'The Light Years' maybe...*

Everyone was smiling at Razmik but he forgot what they

were talking about and what he was going to say.

Then he said: *What were we talking about?*

Yasmin squinted her face.

Leonard said: *I forget.*

Max shook his head. Yasmin said: I *said we can build cities in our bodies, duh.*

Razmik scratched his chin and said: *Right*. He couldn't remember what he'd been going to say.

Everyone waited for him out of kindness, then Leonard said: *This is a fun story...*, but Razmik interrupted, said: *Invisible Cities...* said: *sorry Leonard...* said: *remembered I was going to say Calvino has a book, Invisible Cities...*

They waited. He said again: *Sorry.*

Then he said: *Calvino wrote that cities are like dreams... made of our desires and fears...*

He spread open his palms. Everyone nodded.

Then he said: *They create a perspective, but Calvino called this concealment... he called cities deceitful.*

Yasmin was smiling and kept smiling while she said: *In the pool I felt bliss... I felt atop the city immersed in bliss... did you listen to me within my story, and was your reply a feeling or a thought?*

Razmik had expected everyone was going to spend time reflecting upon the quote he shared. Now a curveball had been pitched to him, he thought, he hesitated, then he answered: *I listened... It was a thought your feeling gave me...* She asked: *And was that thought for my thoughts or for your own?* Razmik kept saying: *...The feeling you gave me gave me a thought, my thought came from your feeling, and my thought can enter into your feelings... reciprocity...* She said, real dry: *Oh ok,* and he said: *I always like talking to you because we usually function through reciprocity...* and she said: *It's your city I imagine Razmik, not Calvino's... do you imagine yourself in Calvino's city or in mine?*

Razmik felt cornered, he smiled because what else.

Razmik said: *I mean... I imagine you like I imagine Calivino, and all people, as cities, like you said, I agree, and I think it's popular and beneficial and historical for people to think of themselves as cities... I like that... and I think it's as dangerous as everything in this world is... glad we're talking about this... I like earlier when you said living as a country... you know... what about this one: damned if you do, damned if you don't... what about that, right...*

Leonard remembered he thinks Razmik is a solid idiot.

Something about the guy, always chatting about whatever little idea he trapped in his head. Leonard thought Razmik, who reads books, he can't read a room worth shit. Being around him he feels barely there. The guy barely survives. Leonard hadn't replied to current messages from Razmik because he couldn't imagine a scenario between just the two of them. Once the guy started talking it was hard to stop him. One night Leonard had told him a personal story about his father just to shut him up. Razmik had loved the story because he's such an emotional punk.

Then he remembered that nothing Razmik does in front of him will be a surprise, since the nature of Razmik is surprise, and his talent is for finding a way to ruin a situation. Leonard doesn't feel he shouldn't have seen Razmik today, since he feels people should have contact with each other, but he does wonder and worry a bit about what he's gotten himself into.

But from politeness Leonard, who had a confident and warm voice, who made words sound important, his voice seeming to others evidence of why this world needs words, Leonard pointed toward Little Tokyo and mentioned its weekly community karaoke. He told the table a story, his fun story he'd brought up earlier, about he and a friend singing karaoke in Little Tokyo one night about two months prior.

He mentioned sake.

He said the friend karaoked an outrageous song. He named the song. No one was familiar with the song, but Leonard guaranteed its outrageousness. He sang an example of the song through a smile on his face.

Everyone knew Leonard was being ridiculous, and charming. He knew it too.

He said: *Look at this...*

Leonard demonstrated how his friend had climbed a pole. He mimed pole climbing, he was great at it. Then he said: *And my friend finished the song while dangling off the pole* [Leonard pretends to dangle from a pole], *singing like a goddamn mad man, like a lunatic, and... that's... that's my dude.*

Leonard said: *I can't trust a person who's afraid to be ridiculous around me.*

Leonard said: *Outside the office I'm always ready for what's ridiculous.*

Then Razmik reflected upon the matter of Leonard perhaps clearly liking him. Leonard liked him alright, he just felt okay not being around him much.

Max had been still as a statue until a waiter dropped off another martini. Then he snapped back into action, took another sip of his martini. One could say Max had a mood that was like a dungeon.

Yasmin, still cozied into Max's body, she told a misadventure karaoke story from her own life, involving she fleeing a stage and crying in a bathroom. Then Leonard told a story about trying to karaoke with his dick once. Then there was laughter from everyone, even Max, who said he and Leonard once karaoked and Max sang better, Leonard agreed, patted him on the back.

Razmik didn't have a karaoke story to share, but he liked being around people who were being happy and weren't being made unhappy by him.

Leonard had been telling a karaoke story set in Taipei while Razmik had been listening and also thinking about how Leonard was describing one of his many business trips. Leonard often took business trips around the world on a company dime. He brings his mother with him to the best cities and longest trips. His story had been about her singing karaoke in Taipei, and no one in the bar liked the song except for Leonard, who thought his mother was a miracle and people were rude. It was adorable how sweet Leonard was to his mother, everyone agreed, including Leonard who wasn't sweet to be seen as sweet, he's just plain sweet, which was wonderful. Leonard said when her karaoke session ended he stood and applauded. He said he loved her because she deserved it.

Razmik thought: *These wonderful people whose wonders I sometimes get to enter inside.*

Then, with no one noticing but himself, Razmik began to

feel deeply dejected.

While Yasmin began a story of a vacation misadventure, which story involved a trip to a hospital, Razmik sat with a frozen smile and a blank stare, there but gone.

He liked hearing the story and being around Yasmin, but his feelings weren't sure what to do. He was hearing but not listening. Razmik felt that, from the table of people, he most identified with Max, probably.

He wondered: *How is Max always so quiet, and yet I think of him as tender?*

He concluded: *Because he's with Yasmin and she loves him, and I never know why she does, but that's for them to know.*

Razmik's chin rested on his fist now, his mouth propped shot. The archetypical thinking man. Leonard told a story about vacationing in Barcelona with his mother, and how when she made a smile in the sand with her toes he cried.

Yasmin replied: *Wonderful!*

Razmik wished he had words and stories that would be beneficial to others and himself. That's what he wanted. He envied the spirit of Yasmin and Leonard, their passions, their lives in general.

His adult years had taught Razmik what hardness is, and he missed being taught joy.

Razmik hoped to find a new plan for himself through his life, one that would bring him eudaimonia... and for tonight this table was a lighthouse during his dark sea journey, he and his friends swam in the night's ocean while the wind kissed their smiles.

Razmik shut his eyes, his lids became a rearview mirror and there went his life, then he felt awful until he opened his eyes and saw his friends. Then he felt only a bit awful, and he wished to escape inside more smiles.

Yasmin smiled at him. He smiled back.

Yasmin and Leonard had a conversation about cultural media popular these days. Razmik avoided such conversations like the plague, since he thought popular media warps people from their essential characteristics, deforms them, turns them into manufactured products, though he liked hearing Yasmin and Leonard share their success stories from inside the warehouse. Once during their conversation Razmik made a single snarky comment which he quickly backed away from. Its tension evaporated while Yasmin and Leonard totally agreed on treasuring the same something whatever.

Their smiles, not for him nor related to details which concerned him, they became Razmik's own smiles on occasion, when now and then their feelings drifted toward him through sheer natural force.

He was a wallflower through the night, until past midnight, when it became the next day, Saturday, which was the day Razmik had left from to arrive here. He thought: *This Saturday began better than this Saturday began before, since now it begins with people.*

He smiled.

The holographic birds of paradise danced thrice more, the longest and most ornate performances occurred through midnight, while a holographic Fela Kuti performed with his band, during which time Yasmin told two of the best stories that Razmik had ever heard.

The topic of Razmik's current life came up through the

night. He dodged the questions he could, certain questions cornered him. His personal life is unrelated to this story except for his despair's mechanics being integral to his own. Certainly he felt himself unrelated to the table of people who had lives better than his.

He's nothing but a pebble on the beach, this Razmik.

When Razmik echoed to Leonard and Yasmin some of the same questions he received, the difference was they had marvelous answers. Their lives were going remarkably well, Razmik noticed. Oh, he noticed. He stared at them, at his hands, at the ground, at the rainforest.

These people with their skills at being happy, their skills seemed to Razmik preferable to his own at being afraid.

Razmik longed to self-actualize the beneficial features of a positive and hopeful perspective. He wanted to have the life he wanted to have, not the life he did.

He thought: *Fulfillment might happen.*

Finally around two in the morning, briefly after Yasmin and Max had left, Razmik heard Leonard say: *It's not as easy as going into the room, entering into NeuroPark... because, well, the central nervous system isn't an easy place...*

He said: *I meditate first.*

He said: *My usual routine is to begin with yoga, then I listen to the sounds of whales in the ocean while eating a light snack, then I meditate, then I sit still for a few minutes, waiting to feel absolutely ready to enter NeuroPark.*

Razmik didn't remember how this topic had been brought up. Had he mentioned it? How drunk was Leonard? Max had been the most drunk person at the table, without a doubt.

Razmik had been thinking about certain recent occurrences from his life.

Razmik and Leonard then hugged through eye contact while Leonard continued, glad as always to be telling about his NeuroPark, Razmik glad to hear: *I go in absolutely clear headed because what's in my head becomes my reality... what happens is a cerebral reality forms from my imagination... like holographic virtual reality, but I'm the engineer of what I see... and the place I'm in changes with my thoughts...*

Razmik had some questions: *What do you mean? How long does this happen? What do you do?*

Leonard told him: *I travel across the world I want to be in, and do more of what I want to do, for as long as I want to...*

Razmik thought about this. Then he said: *Sounds like your life to me anyway.*

Leonard let out a hearty laugh.

Leonard said: *Close but not quite... I guess this way it's more fantastic than real... but it feels as real as the fantastic can...*

They both become quiet. Razmik because he thought about what Leonard said. Leonard because he loved how people became quiet when he told them about NeuroPark.

Leonard said: *It's what we've always wanted, of course, as a technology, our dreams our reality, and now it's a thing...*

He said: *The purpose of modern human advancement has been to create our wants.*

Leonard asked: *Isn't that wonderful?*

Razmik said it was, but he wasn't sure.

Then on their way to Leonard's skyscraper penthouse, where his mother was sleeping, while Leonard was drunk happy, and Razmik was uncommonly happy, they walked across the Santa Monica Strip with life in their eyes and hearts, out among the late-night crowd who are within their own fights too.

The late-night crowd always dreams and fights, if not for the next day for the next night, their bodies vessels filled by the joy they create.

Razmik considered moving back to Los Angeles, which still he didn't think of as any better than Kolkata, but he didn't know anyone there like Yasmin or Leonard, and he wondered if perhaps people are more important than places.

He told this to Leonard, who smiled hugely, motivating Razmik to smile as well.

Leonard, lying a tad, said he'd treasure the event of Razmik moving back to Los Angeles. He said: *You belong here!* Leonard said: *Wait until you experience NeuroPark... wait until you feel and live your life as you want it!*

That morning Razmik's life, which felt different to him then, it actually was what it always was, it was his life, but what changes this story is he and Leonard never made it to where they were headed, for certain reasons outside this story which has ended.

Cotton Candy

Then he flies backwards, smacks and shakes a wall, he's on his back, then he's on his knees, then he's on his feet escaping from the art museum.

Beneath the sun, again his life doesn't change based on his predictions, since life changes by its own accord, and while falling into the sky he whispers *Of course,* as if he always knew this was next.

He's familiar with the feeling of falling up. He arrives to rest on a cloud. The sun kisses his eyelids. The wind whispers secrets. Then he's back on the ground, specifically, he's returned to the art museum.

Detail: a man in an art museum opens his eyes. Other eyes around the room look down on him. Hands are on his shoulders. He begins to rise and hands keep him down. He blinks, he blinks. His head's interior swirls. He touches his back which, to this surprise, doesn't hurt. How did he fall? Here he is on the ground. Other hands not his own are on his shoulders, he wiggles, wiggles, he fights being down, he fights against hands which finally release him.

A man in an art museum opens his eyes and his name is Ricardo. He's on his feet then he falls back down. He hears from around the room *Oh no... Again, oh no...*

Everyone's eyes... there they all are... those eyes on Ricardo. *Is this how I'll be remembered?* he wonders and he blinks, he blinks.

Perhaps the difference between being seen and being remembered is testing me now... He thinks while he wishes to rise, but other hands keep him down. He doesn't feel panicked, no, he feels sure that he shall not panic.

Now he stays quiet, except for answering *Yes/No* questions, then time passes by terror, then Ricardo goes to stand, wobbles, his eyes close, his head smacks against the ground.

Now, later: his eyes open to a few other eyes. Some heads shake in the background. Someone is on a phone, calling for an ambulance. He feels a dark weight within his head. A coarse hand touches his cheek. He wishes no other eyes nor heads were here, he wishes the same for himself.

Then, *I shall stand,* he thinks, and...

The following day he reflected upon what transpired but chose to forget during some moments, for example when he sat at the tea bar counter.

Ricardo was familiar with the employees of this neighborhood tea bar, Life Spoiler, which he regularly visited. While his eyes absorbed Life Spoiler's panorama he shared some nods and smiles with some people he knew.

That day Ricardo was meeting a detective, Tony, since a friend of a friend figured they two, Ricardo and Tony, would lace as people.

(They shall not lace.)

Ricardo was curious about Tony who was a detective. The detective profession belonged to people who, unable to solve their own problems, they solve other people's problems. Their analytics submerge personhood and swell reality into dis-human proportions, called facts. In Ricardo's opinion facts were for buzzards. Facts to him existed as emotions which were known only to each person, and the purity of the subjective was his belief. All beauty comes from or involves emotions, he knew.

Live action: Tony's eyes on Ricardo's spider leg fingers.

Ricardo's anxiety wiggled his fingers and while Tony smiled Tony wished he hadn't agreed to this arrangement.

Tony spotted not a horrible night but one he didn't need.

Then their eyes were on each other, and Ricardo wanted his eyes elsewhere, so Tony began to stare at eyes which no longer stared back... but then: typical conversational endeavors transpired, such as questions regarding each other, this portion being omitted from the story by the writer on account of interior selves being but thrusters astride this jet of a narrative which flies through clouds of small moments without looking back.

Now, later, their heads titled back, they each stared at the ceiling until their eyes closed. And then they each left Life Spoiler, without ever meeting each other again.

But: again it's a Tuesday which maybe wasn't Tuesday, but definitely what maybe happened was, is, or will be, that during Ricardo's falling problems, back at the art museum, back then Fernando had had the most interesting story from the collection of people, actually, if you think about it, in my opinion, since Fernando demonstrated through his choices and actions that living with a life perspective preserved in altruism enables the possibility of hope being restored to the reality of the human experience. With the possibility of hopes comes the possibility of anything!

Nice, Fernando. *Nice.* Fernando from Hadleyburg, he fell into some money and he didn't spend it. He always lived in the same studio apartment. When anyone asked him about his money, he then asked them about their money. He did that. Results were varied. It's a personal question. What the person was able to do, without knowing they could, as Fernando asked those he helped not to tell others he had, the person was able to consider how much money they needed to live how they wanted to live, they were asked to truly consider and ask for that amount, if that was within them, which sometimes it wasn't (there's more variation to human possibility than sometimes given credit), and Fernando was always open to what he heard, always ready to be there. Which seems crazy. He was a *rara avis*.

Fernando had stipulated, to himself, that two was the total number of times a person could ask him for money, with maybe an exception for some third times, depending, but definitely not four, probably (it happened).

Example: Oliver from Grand Rapids, not realizing his situation with Fernando didn't require business talk, not able to unglue himself from the ideas the money gave him, Oliver told Fernando he absolutely saw the national cultural need for an extravagant water park lined with neon and open only at night. Club City... there's where he wanted to be so there's where he wanted to bring others. Fernando gave Oliver ten million dollars and Oliver built Club City, which became as successful as Oliver had described it would.

Following Club City's colossal success the idea of Las Vegas as the holy place for adult fantasy became a tired dream. Las Vegas was sacked as Rome had been sacked, not from one but by a series... the perception grew that fantasy could be wherever you made it and however you did. An American Amsterdam landed in Indiana, Portland became a Berlin (its destiny), all of the South became like all of Italy and in fact Orlando became small potatoes. Disney World hadn't been enough!

Now Ricardo is back in Life Spoiler. Today he's extra-aware

of everyone's facial hair and hair lines. Also, mannerisms. *Better watch those*, he thinks. He counts fold lines on people's faces. He looks at arm hair. He's remembering his day here with Tony. *That was ridiculous*, he remembers. He doesn't feel afraid of himself but knows he feels doomed and knows he must not let his feelings of doom become his reality. Life Spoiler looks like trash, he thinks, he thinks this place is faded and dying and it's trash but he sits down and decides not to let today worry him.

I'd rather be trash than not be anything, he thinks. He orders his tea and eggs from Babs and he knows there's another way to look at things.

His thoughts spin and collect in his head like cotton candy in a machine.

Insect Fantasy

I've been a butterfly for a while now, who cares. My wings have been my wings for as long as they have, some number of days, some Mondays to Sundays to Mondays again.

It's my remembrances of being a caterpillar which cause me to feel a primordial togetherness with an eternal universe of change. A reality of metamorphosis, here I am, a bodily manifestation of transformation.

While I was a larva, I didn't have any real problems. Being immature was rad. I liked eating as much as I wanted to. I ate more than anyone I knew. When my chrysalis arrived I was huge, which means there was more of life, more beauty. During my days of being a pupa I knew I was becoming the butterfly I was becoming. I'd heard about my natural cycle. Before I had my wings I knew: *there'll be my wings*. When I saw my wings I loved them but I wasn't astonished. I was an instant flapper, sure. Life all the time! OBVIOUS. So here my wings are yet I'm the same, yet different. I've gone from crawling to flying. I don't have any real problems being a butterfly either, but that's because I was once a caterpillar, I always remember.

When I tell this to my friend, one day while she and I flap our wings and mouths, she says that's one way to think about it. She mentions another: her family is ludicrous, so life is absolutely ludicrous. She mentions this twice along with further explanations.

She says she'd rather be a flower as she lands on one. Then a child chases or plays with her under the sun, and *that's a butterfly's life* when the child steps on the flower where my friend is.

Tears falling from my eyes to my wings, I fly to other flowers.

At night while I don't let the wind shake me, in a slow motion dark world I feel alive and miss my friend. My next day stares at me. Her death haunts me. Our final moment plays on repeat in my memories. She *was* real. I *am* real. I'm not a caterpillar any longer, chill, and I must remember one day I won't be a butterfly either.

From being a caterpillar to being a butterfly to being dead. This fast world, this short life. *While I'm alive I'll feel alive*, the butterfly thinks, remembering a song he'd heard from a car window one country night (back when he was a caterpillar).

Nature Fantasy

Hank learned to live with 100% hope. That's one way to do it.

In his current life stage Hank desires to be around flowers, constantly. He wants it to be that each day of his life he sees a flower (which makes him smile).

So what'd he do he planted a pack of seeds in his garden.

I'm a seed among a hundred planted in the front yard of Hank's house.

Factors of our well-being and futures depend on how Hank treats us, of course, how we were planted and how we'll be tended. 70% of seeds germinate under suitable conditions for growth.

Yet I wish not to speak of how nature nor Hank treat me, for I do not control how they control me.

Do I fear that I shall not become alive? My flowering is a separate conversation from I being this seed.

Oh, I'm planted far too deeply. I know for sure. I don't exist in a situation which fosters growth. I don't deny this, no, it's that my fears aren't my delight.

Some seeds have already germinated into fabulous angiosperms. Some of them make me cry they are so beautiful! How nice it must be to stretch and look above the soil.

Near me are others who have not yet grown. They and I, we remember all that begins ends. Stuck inside darkness we are sometimes quiet, and on our worst days we think *Here is the time we have, how we have it, okay...*

There is more in a day than time! Somehow it's true...

There is more than the fact of me maybe being a seed which shall not grow!

Fuck!

Some may describe life in the sky they stretch to see, and I shall describe worms and soil (which worms and soil can describe themselves, but not from the seed's perspective).

[Omitted section about worms and soil.]

After I have not life my nothingness will expand into forever. Forever nothing, yes, and the concept of forever is unrelated to me. Existence exists without me and clocks don't know of me, the universe doesn't need me. I was here because I was and that's what happened.

Sorry. I *am* here and that's what *is* happening. I feel the soil around me. The seed next to me just cracked upon and I believe in its future, and I believe my today is my today for what it's worth.

What of Hank who watches, whom I'll never make smile, that's a bummer, literally not a smile, his hope for me his own.

Harold Harold Harold

Harold's roommate said it was a bad idea, but Harold wasn't afraid of his roommate's opinions, he wasn't afraid of anybody but himself, and right now he thought he was being a rebel, and hilarious, and foul, a few of his favorite things, and he replied to his roommate that he *don't give a fuck about nothing*.

He left his apartment building and entered the porta potty across the street. He stood on the toilet and as his ass hovered the floor he first retched a gigantic fart then he took a colossal shit. Created a real ugly, unfortunate mess. His shit *splattered* across the floor. So he sprayed his shit all over the floor of this porta potty in order to make a social protest against the reason this porta potty was there outside this lot for use by the construction workers building the condominium replacing the building which some neighborhood flyers mentioned was probably historic. Harold knew that it was the business world which was truly disgusting.

His eyes scanned for toilet paper.

He should've planned ahead his toilet paper situation.

He hadn't planned this shit protest.

In this plan's developmental phase, while his stomach was suggesting oncoming trouble, he had told his roommate he was going to the porta potty because he didn't want to make their own toilet *messy*. The roommate had said *there must be another way*. Enough about the roommate and the context.

How am I going to reach the toilet paper, Harold wondered.

He daintily stepped onto the floor, reached for the toilet paper dispenser, his pants around his ankles, his right hand holding his pants up to his thighs, but he found only a lone and final toilet paper sheet, a single one, and then, related to personal frustration, he turned his head to scream, and while he screamed his foot slipped and his face wiped against his diarrhea on the floor.

He pushed himself up with his hands but his hands slipped on his shit and his face wiped the floor again. *Outrageous*, he thought. This situation became so overwhelming that he in fact crawled inside the porta potty toilet seat and into the land of shit.

He walked around in there, and everyone was nice, but he knew they were actual shit. They didn't talk to him through their shit grins, of course not, but sonorous/conversational farts did emit from their insides. They weren't that bad. He made a couple of friends and lots of suspicions.

Then after he climbed a vine into the sky of shit land he returned to reality but he was surprised when leaving the porta potty to find the cops had surrounded him owing to his ruckus.

Thankfully, his roommate was a solid person.

Knowing the bad would arrive to Harold he'd prepared a backup plan of good.

A rope appeared in front of Harold's eyes.

He saw it. He looked up. There was his roommate, flying his helicopter.

The roommate's helicopter caused the cops to whip out

their guns. The neighbors pulled out their eyes. The sunset kissed the sky orange and purple and Harold grabbed the rope ladder and climbed it while the helicopter began to rise.

Harold laughed at the cops who were tiny and away from him while he was inside the helicopter.

His roommate mentioned, *You look-smell like shit.*

Harold had heard worse. He high-fived his roommate.

And when they high-fived the roommate by accident he smashed the helicopter into a palm tree and later in the hospital Harold wished he'd never gotten them both into that situation. His roommate was dead. Why'd that have to happen? *Bogus.* What's going to be his quadriplegic living situation, he wondered this and other things, then he left the hospital after two years of recovery, and for three years he worked as a quadriplegic detective in New York City. Everyone was ready to share their secrets with him, yes.

Then one day while in a taxi a hot air balloon landed on the street and Harold's taxi swerved and crashed against a concrete barrier, and he died but the taxi driver was okay and Harold had been headed to LAX to fly to Thailand for reasons unrelated to this story.

[Wiki for Developmental robotics] Starting from the essential idea that learning and development happen as the self-organized result of the dynamical interactions among brains, bodies and their physical and social environment, and trying to understand how this self-organization can be harnessed to provide task-independent lifelong learning of skills of increasing complexity, developmental robotics strongly interacts with fields such as developmental psychology, developmental and cognitive neuroscience, developmental biology (embryology), evolutionary biology, and cognitive linguistics.

Fractal Fiction

Recently he'd been conspiratorial on a number of topics which, after conspiring upon them, suddenly (how all the best thoughts arrive, same as the worst), he thought he figured something out, and he thought his figuring out opened his eyes to fabulous realizations

stoking a fire inside himself, power-flames

further conspiring

He became a conspiracy theorist from an emotional perspective

thinking there was a goddamn thing about the world which he could see and understand and be a part of

He figured out [redacted] and [redacted] and a pterodactyl.

First of all who is that?

I realize next to me is myself, whom I didn't recognize because I never have before, only dreamed I could.

There I am and here I am and that's something else. What will I say to myself? My other me's face doesn't move. Why is that? And do I know I know I'm wondering, I wonder. What? My other face doesn't move. I don't know what to do with myself, and that's so typical. All the options. There I am, why don't I do something? That's what I should know to do! What a calamity,

[other me slyly smiles]

Pause. A short beat. An intermission from anything... the stillness of silence and nothing but thoughts, feelings...

What the fuck do I know that I'm not telling myself?? My smile, its mystery! This is utter disaster

[other me's head tilts]

Nah... I mean

fool me twice, shame on me. Either way we're clearly in a bad situation.

My thoughts and feelings become vibratory. I transmit frequencies of despair

not going to let myself be judged by sassy faces any longer.

Then I, the real me, I already know (discover within myself) that other-I didn't judge me, that other-I responded to fear with a concerned face, just that, and the overall intention was for visible fears to become fears we can conquer.

How am I thinking that and what is happening? I walk toward myself, I smile, my pupils dilate as if I'm happy to see me. When I look into the mirror I don't often like seeing myself, so I think this situation feels unrealistic and I don't know why it's happening. I look at myself and other-I begins to talk as if the mood is light:

You're so young. I appear to you as you, that's because of surgeries and inventions. Tomorrow I, you, turn sixty-five. I plan to die tomorrow, so I decided to come back and see myself at this point. This day's important because it's the day I visit myself, which I always guessed I would. Of course it's not literally a big deal.

Because I'm not, totally, listening to myself, I say *Huh?*

I stare at myself and don't know what the hell

So I stare at myself staring at myself without knowing what the hell. Two faces represent this same emotion. Two faces which are the same face but not but are.

When other-I said *plan* and *die* that felt a little dark.

from my mouth, yes, I know what I meant

what's your favorite food?

Chicken, I think-say, then other-I shakes my head and says *So young...*

I'm going to stop eating meat, aren't I? Myself I'm nodding.

Not-I laughs and says:

Yes, you're right about that, yes, that is funny, yes, thank you for mentioning that, since always sometimes when I begin to talk with other people it can be hard for me to remember everything at once, you know, my eyes search within their eyes and I become lost, always, yes, other eyes aren't my eyes so, sure, that's a pickle, most of the time when my thoughts travel inside a person I lose the topic I came in with, almost as if, well, yes, almost as if my thoughts are my soul's tour guide but my tour guide doesn't know about being outside of me, maybe, what, Grace, maybe, obvious, sweet girl, my good friend who will listen to me this day while I'm in absolute hysterics, I thought you were me for a moment!, yes it's true, I shouldn't admit it but I did admit it because I'm glad to see you, oh, yes, I just realized, just now, I realized that you're you, I felt wonderful!, I feel wonderful, yes, most glad, thank you for being you, thank you for laughing with me!, thank you for making me laugh today, even hysterical laughter is better than no laughter, is that true, hey, returning back to before I started saying this... this, me saying this, has it maybe made us lose the place from where we came, that's my uj, my kind of bad, my bad for sure Grace, whom I never mean to lead astray, no, we are headed into our futures and that's where we'll like to be, yes, that's where I'll find you, maybe, maybe because who knows, who knows if we'll stay friends, my dove, since life gets shaken up and we stir around inside it, you know, me, I know at any rate that I run circles in a cage of windows and that's my life, there's a side-fact, an analogy no is it visual symbolism no am I lost again wait yes I spin inside a closed place which makes me see myself, every day, every moment, do you think that too, Grace, now or ever do you think that too, sorry, side-question, sorry, okay we were talking about how The Inclusionary Society (of which I'm a member), they're about to hold an international convention that's expected to attract over forty-five countries I hear, I heard that, that forty-six other countries will be at... this, wait, yes, forty-eight countries will be there and it's going to be a big event, it'll be a big deal, absolutely, it's destined to be great, and meaningful, yes, powerful, right, it'll be a culturally shapeshifting international convention that'll have fifty-five different countries represented and over a thousand attendees, easily, over double-digit thousands, probably triple, who knows, maybe, you don't want to jinx it, one can't say for sure but there might be a million people, though I can say there should be at least one-hundred million!, because TIS of Los Angeles has the belief that humans can accept themselves and others, mmhmm, every type of person can be themselves, my dove, since each person is a wonderful and magical being, I try to remember that, how we're pieces of human from nature, Grace, remember, remember the thing about we being stardust, you know, that's a good one isn't it, do you think that's a good one Grace, do you, because if you don't then I won't either and nevermind, nevermind, okay this convention will discuss the future living possibilities of all of Earth's citizens, yeah, the whole population, sure: all different types of people, how are they going to get along with each other, how are they going to do it, this the topic TIS discusses, that's what they chat about, okay, okay for a

moment I forgot, not this, but what I was going to say
about it and, wait, I forget, I forget but hold your horses
because I remember I was saying: so humans can let each
person be who they are, that'll be a byproduct of people
liking themselves, yeah, the belief is that if each person
allows themselves to be themselves this will allow them to
allow others to be themselves, right, and through accepting
themselves and others what'll evaporate is this constant
fear humans have of other humans, yes, Grace, who listens
to me with such sweetness, my dove, I'm referring to that
ridiculous problem where not only do humans not know for
sure what has brought them into existence but they can't
exist

a galaxy which doesn't govern itself by the narratives we
create while living here, our lives indeed our imaginations,
that's the human condition and, well, Grace, I should
mention this, my dove, that the galaxy doesn't have a
human condition, nah, hey do you like potato chips, here
are some potato chips I thought I'd mention that now, okay,
okay the convention, okay my life, life, it's this nightmare,
everyone lives in this nightmare called life, everyone does,
so sometimes it doesn't matter, don't you feel it doesn't
matter, sometimes, do you feel that, is that just me, no, no
I don't think it is even if you might say so, because some
things that happen we don't want to say

our cycle around the sun, big whoop, but, so, TIS says life
can be a big deal, yes, feel big

A miraculous feeling overtakes one when the world becomes
what one had thought the world might become.

Things become miraculous indeed, that's science. Happens.
In ancient days

oblivious

except, core human

demonstrates that within reality the observable can alter
itself into a form which comes as if from a dream. The Big

Bang to now. Did The Big Bang see me coming? The Big Bang thought not of me but of everyone.

To repeat: The Big Bang thought of everyone.

The Inclusionary Society of Los Angeles, California, which assembled itself in 2020, and is now semi-famous, but not too famous since most people don't care about facts, TIS was the first American-established community to think out loud that the best possible course toward future planetary existence was an overall acceptance of the absolute numerical mania of living potentials within human and robot futures.

Since Anything Can Happen, Anything Can Be Believed was their proclamation.

affective neuroscience

standard ideals of Utopia were scientifically emotional, and emotions warp science warp life warp

acknowledging that emotions characterize the reality of being human, and TIS used to say *Live It, Love it.*

TIS believed in the "everlasting possibilities of human endeavors and achievements which carry neither name nor flag nor bear responsibility for any person to behave in any way which does not suit them."

Any person can be any type of person was their guiding philosophy. At first their numbers had been small, then they'd grown into numbers which,

So many ways to be a person

an ideal, one way to do things,

boring

Everyone was afraid of each other. No one knew who they were.

Only some things had made any sense

there was better

[*Reconsolidation: Or, it's the ghosts who will answer you*] In my dreams I catch myself spying on myself, I become the ghost haunting myself, as I wander through dream-worlds, unraveling threads and unable to really touch anything, but I follow and watch and see what the memories do to my body, what they do to me.

Having disrobed himself of obsessive self-awareness, which had amplified his egomaniacal tendencies, there he was in the jungle. There he was in the jungle. He looked around and wondered of all the names he didn't know for all the things he could see. What were the words for those present odors? He chose not worry about the words he smelled. No one else around him, names meant nothing. His fingers brushed the wild. He didn't have to think about this being real for it to be. He wasn't the creator of all around him, everywhere, each thing its own life. And what, then, were his thoughts of? Zero wondering. One step forward into sensation. An animal. Living for survival. There he was in the jungle, within a nature which was his for now.

On a Scale of One to Ten

It's almost troubling how comfortable it all feels. Like, like it's not happening, and at the same time like, of course it's this, of course this is happening, has happened. Either I'm dead, or this is a turning point. But either way there's a sense of ease, a naturalness that swept over me at some point. I guess it could have been the moment I bounced off the side of that car. I just didn't notice the change right away because of the chaos. Everyone else was moving so much. The people on the street, standing above me on Hollywood Blvd., the paramedics with questions and instructions and fingers to follow with eyes and directions for muscles not to move.

When I got to LA County General, neck braced in plastic and too many thoughts about internal bleeding, there were more questions, a lot of laying around, and more people fussing over me or other people. There were screams and beeps and doctor speak and vibrating moans. I was very worried about me. There was adrenaline, shock and after-shock and injections and scans, being rolled from one bed to another bed and back, etc. General ER stuff.

I've never before seen so many square feet of bland ceiling. To recount what had happened, the accident, is not as straightforward as everyone wants it to be. I could tell, could hear a certain disappointment or frustration, was able to find the same tones in each different voice that asked the same questions, each one equal also to the last in the way they seemed to be paying no attention to my answers. I didn't fault anyone; not even the lady who hit me—accidents happen (but I do hope she has insurance), and for those first few hours I was even in a pretty good mood.

A team of doctors and nurses hovered around me, poking, cutting, taping, smearing jelly on my abdomen and looking through me with ultrasonic devices. Satisfied that I was in no immediate danger, even satisfying my own morbid hypochondria, someone called them away to bay 12 where the blood was flowing more rapidly, I heard something about a head on collision, about high speeds and an air lift. "You got really lucky." A disembodied voice told me. The first of many times I would hear those words over the next four days. I knew that was true, even then when I still wasn't sure what the total damage was, but at the same time I thought; It's a hard and thankless job, being the lucky one. When everything hurts and feels pretty damn scary and everyone's always rushing off to help someone else who got less lucky.

Someone stepped up to my bedside, just out of sight, tied off my arm and started injecting something. "Fentanyl, for the pain," they told me when I asked what it was. "Is that the new thing everybody's ODing on in the streets," I questioned. "No, I think you're thinking of heroin." To myself: "Nope. Pretty sure I know what heroin is. And I'm a little worried about you being in the medical profession if you're not even hip to what opioid epidemics are out there." Then they wheeled me off to stare at the same ceiling of a different hallway, to be forgotten about for twenty or thirty minutes (which I've come to realize is part of the medical handbook, may even be a whole chapter in *Gray's Anatomy*), and giving me the program for the day in jargon (I'm taking you to CT then you'll see ortho in recess 5, if you're lucky, they'll decide if you're NPO or if you can be released today). I thought about asking for clarification but fell asleep instead.

"I don't know. I just got back and they told me he needed a scan." These words from the upside-down whiskered mouth of a pudgy faced man who was leaning over me. I could see his nipples were hard, or maybe just long, casting small shadows on his scrubs. "Well can you look at the work order because they told me it was for head, chest and pelvis, but they also told me they sent you a work order and you would know." This, unfortunately, was not the first or last of the situations in which I would have to utilize breathing techniques and eye closing to keep me from freaking out about how uncommunicative everyone seems to be. I breathed deep, noticing how truly uncomfortable the neck brace was and hoping it would soon be removed.

They two gathered the sheets around me, sliding my body from one hard chunk of plastic to another. Before disappearing, the technician mumbled something about injections and heat and remaining still. I wasn't even entirely sure he was talking to me or if he was still jawing with the nurse who would forget me in several more hallways before the day was over. I felt wiggling and pulling, something being attached to the iv port that had been temporarily installed in my left arm during the ambulance ride, then the sound of a door closing. I was contemplating the large plastic porthole in the middle of which I was suspended, thinking it looked more like an oversized fisher price play set than a hundreds of thousands of dollars piece of science, when the fire started moving through me. From my arm to my chest, up to the head and down to the pelvis, it was just a warm oozing at first and I thought this must be the heated injection the technician had mentioned. But as my interior rapidly moved toward burning I let out a holler of a question

— "Is it supposed to feel like, hot hot?" There was no human answer, but the fisher price machine gave a little jolt, instructing me to hold my breath or release, as it moved through its stages of photographing my insides.

It was hard to get a definite answer from anyone. After each test I asked how things looked. A general response would be to deflect to the doctors. Nurses and techs saying that they simply administer the tests and that I would have to wait to hear results from the doctors. Doctors would say I was lucky, but more tests were needed, along with time, to see how things would play out. I wanted to tell them that they were the lucky ones. To not be injured, and to have jobs that seemed not to require any specific knowledge or skill. My frustration had begun. Would continue to build over the next two days.

That's when my girlfriend showed up. I had called her, head resting on my backpack as a pillow, trying to keep my body from writhing while I waited for the ambulance to pick my up from my position in the street. Her face moved into my fixed view of ceiling as she took my hand and tried to smile. Bending over me, head backlit, face in shadow, shallow tears building in the corners of her eyes, I felt relief. Short lived, as they tied off my arm and began the slow process of extracting an amount of blood that felt like too much, my arm going numb below the tourniquet, heart rate increasing as vials were filled with plasma I didn't care to part with. But she was there. And she was on my side. I've never wanted to rely on someone else for my own piece of mind, but sometimes it's nice to be able to defer that burden to trusted shoulders.

"On a scale of one to ten, where would you rate your pain?" I had been in room 116 on the sixth floor orthopedic wing for about two hours, on hospital grounds for seven, it was 7:15pm and I hadn't had anything to eat or drink since around six in the morning, when Kailyn had left for work and I poured myself a cup of coffee and a bowl of Kroger Crunchy Raisin Bran in coconut milk. Almost all of those words would not have applied to me a week ago. But Kailyn and I had moved in together and the pantry (a word I've heretofore never used when talking about food in my kitchen) was stock full of all sorts of new items.

When they moved me to my private room it'd been ten hours since I'd had anything to drink and no one but me seemed concerned about my dehydration. Having brought this fact up several times, the doctors and nurses brushed past it, saying that I would probably be going into surgery at any moment. I had gone from being released same day to ready for surgery at a moment's notice. It seemed that I had a fracture that was exposed at the joint through a tear in the skin of my ankle. Also, a fractured spine, which they told me was small, inconsequential, that there was nothing they could do about it anyway. The neurosurgeon told me it was actually quite common and nothing to be worried about.

"I used to be friends with a few life guards and they always had stories about people who hit their heads on sandbars and stuff at the beach, chipping off a small piece of vertebrae which, late that night or the next, as they lay in bed sleeping, would creep around and sever the spinal cord, causing paralysis and stuff. Can you just tell me that won't happen to me," I asked. He looked at me, like he was going to say something, before deciding on "I'm positive that won't happen to you. That piece of bone, not even really near the spinal cord, is surrounded by a bunch of muscle tissue and, seriously, I see these things every day and I've never heard of what you're talking about happening." That made me feel better. But it was the last time anyone wearing scrubs would bring up anything besides my ankle.

The ankle wasn't even hit by the car, I don't think. I was for sure hit on the left side, direct shot to the kidney, probably with the side mirror, which caused me to spin down the passenger side, basically pummeling my whole body and making every inch of me sore as fuck. I waited for surgery in a very bleak, white room with a tiny tv, Kailyn and my parents (who arrived a couple hours after I surrendered to their need to be involved) at my bedside. Everything was really stressing me out by this point. I was pretty sure I wouldn't get out of surgery until the next day, which meant an overnight stay in a hospital, that I hadn't planned and which, frankly, really put a damper on finishing the move and settling in to the new place. Not to mention the book of short stories I was working on.

The service at LA County General, overall, was terrible. Even if the hospital employees, on the whole, were pleasant and seemed to be trying their best. I don't know if it was planned, but they informed me that I wouldn't be going into surgery until the next day and followed that news with a shot of morphine and something to prevent nausea. The morphine didn't ease the pain, but it did give me a powerful full body ache that was at least a change of pace from the pain up to that point. I looked out my single square window which aligned perfectly with the single square window of a room directly across the way in a different wing. The man inhabiting that room seemed as displeased as me, if not a little more unhinged.

"Your king died." The attendant's voice was deep and thick with the accent of an African nation. "Right. Your king died. Everybody so sad. You sad?" He was pushing me through the series of endless hallways and corridors that would eventually lead to the operating room. I couldn't be bothered to turn my head, as I was too busy worrying about all the warnings related to surgery and anesthesia, the long list of potential mishaps I'd consented to chance. But near as I could tell, he was talking to a Thai co-worker regarding the recent death of their beloved leader. The Thai man was walking along with us, the two of them chatting back and forth, seeming not to be listening to each other but conversing, either out of a need to break up the monotony or a sense of duty toward cordiality.

"Yes. It was a sad day. We are all sad."

"Who will take his place. Who will be your new king?"

"The prince. But people do not like him."

"Who? The prince? When will he be king? Why don't they like him?"

"Yes. They think he is a playboy. He is sad. He will mourn for a year."

"A year! That is too long. A year! No my friend. A year is too long. He is young. All that money and power... surrounded by women... of course he will have his faults..."

"He is young. Still, the people do not like him. I do not like him. He is not his father. And he is not so young. Sixty or Sixty five."

They said their goodbye's as we bumped over the threshold of an elevator, me hoping that I'd soon be under, regardless of the consequences. I felt tired. Super tired. And sick of having such a dry mouth. It had been thirty hours since I'd had anything to eat or drink. They'd pushed a couple bags of saline through my iv but my piss was still a vibrant orange each time I drained the ounce or two of myself I could muster into the rifle-butt-shaped-plastic-pee-bottle that none of the nurses would bother to empty and my tongue was developing ridges to rival a wavy potato chip.

In one of the adjacent curtained bays of an operating room that could double as a basement level telemarketing office, I listened to the head anesthesiologist go through the rigmarole speech she would soon be giving to me. Each sentence ending with a pause at which point it was translated to Spanish for a patient who seemed even more concerned than I was about the aspects of the procedure that end, potentially, in death. Although I couldn't make out all the questions, the panic in the voice was easily discerned and began to raise the heart rate I had struggled, fairly successfully thus far, to control.

I thought about the Thai king. Less than a week earlier, it would have been Saturday I guess, the first day Kailyn and I had started moving into our new apartment in Franklin Village or Little Armenia or Los Feliz (not pronounced philes) depending on who you talk to, my dad was helping with some of the heavier furniture and we took a break for lunch before dropping him at Union Station. In Thai Town, seated at a patio table at the Shrimp Lover, a Thai/Cajun restaurant that Kailyn worked at for three plus years, a waitress greeted us and, in response to a jovial question from my dad about how her day was going she replied, "Our king is dead." Solemnly.

We talked about it after lunch. How, if I were in another country, even just on vacation, and someone told me that an American political dignitary had died, I probably wouldn't even remember it the next day. Certainly the news wouldn't spoil my vacation. And here this woman was, living thousands of miles removed from that place, from that king, affected on an emotional level. And now evidence of someone else, equally distressed under similar circumstances. I was wondering about these things, probably in an attempt to keep my mind from the immediate, when the anesthesiologist and her unit arrived at my bedside.

She asked me questions, again warning me of all the potential mortality risks, giving me a play by play of how things would go down, handing me a pen and more paperwork to sign and initial, telling me she'd be back in a moment with something to calm my nerves, which I'd expressly stated had become a bit on edge. I don't know why I was so nervous exactly. Surely my body had been put through more turmoil over the years than what lay ahead of me. But they really hammer home how many ways things can go wrong during and after the surgery. And maybe it was exactly because I'd already survived so much in my life that it seemed logical, or at least plausible, that none of that—car accident included, would kill me, but a simple ankle incision would.

The last thing I remember was a green rubber mask (which I'd been told was oxygen) being put over my face. Watching the green elastic stretch at the place where it attached to the mask. I don't remember a smell. In fact, I don't know if I remember any smells from any point after the accident up to that point. Maybe I do remember them, just not like, right now.

I came to in the same curtained partition of the telemarketers basement where I'd gone under. Things were wobbly, the way a director might try to portray p.o.v. drunkenness. I know I asked questions: when would I be back in my room (maybe even meaning at home), how did the operation go. But being still alive was enough comfort in that moment. It was however, the first of several times I would contemplate whether or not I was in fact still alive or if this was something else, somewhere else, or even that I might be someone else. It remains unclear whether or not these were the right questions to ask or what their answers are.

Eventually I was back in the bland room I had been assigned the previous evening. I believe Kailyn and my parents and her mom were there. There were people present. I don't remember the return journey in the least but it must have been similarly long and boring, through the maze of designless, colorless corridors that exists to create a sense of cleanliness but really only exacerbate an emotional tone of filth. To me at least.

That day went by. Kailyn and her mom left, my parents spent the night. I think I ate an apple. Or, no, my parents brought me a sandwich. I was bothered by everyone. Nurses came in at irregular intervals that made the interruptions seem constant. The only benefit being that fifty percent of the time they gave me drugs. The pain was severe, in the ankle especially, but really throughout my back and body. Drugs dulled the muscle aches, but as one of the nurses, Ang, told me, "Bone pain is bone pain. It's just gonna hurt. That's pretty much it." Morphine and Fentanyl weren't really doing shit and Kailyn's mom, a nurse, had asked them to try Dilaudid which I liked better, due in part to the weird hurt that came with it.

With the plastic iv ports securely taped into each arm, they would screw on and push a little saline flush through before and after each injection. It wasn't until the after-shot flush when I would feel a discomfort pour through me. It was a visceral feeling of an amount of liquid just a little too thick for my veins being forced through them. And the high wasn't all that noticeable, in such small doses at least (or based on the fact that I already had quite a reserve of drugs built up over the last 48hrs), but in the case of all the future injections, I waited for that second shot of saline, a little giddy for the hurt which I now characterized in my minds eye as a little steamroller paving the way for the okay feeling.

People came and went from the room. My phone was always somewhere nearby but I rarely remembered it or found any interest there. The sheets were never changed, the room was never cleaned. I went through moods. Sometimes I was angry at everyone and thought I was justified in being so. Or I was cordial, genuinely not having that bad of a time. Other times I would reply brusquely, then rescind my comments and offer my apologies, thinking I was right to be angry but wrong to express it. I refused most of the hospital food unless it looked fresh-ish and easily digestible. There was nothing worth watching on tv but I still flipped through the channels a few times a day. Once, I made a joke about Julia

Childs and I swear to god, like three hours later, they were replaying old episodes of her show on PBS. I didn't say so out loud but this was one of the times I wondered about my living/deadness.

I had started reading Shirley Jackson's *We Have Always Lived in the Castle* a couple days prior to the incident, having been given a copy I found as a duplicate while working for a friend, helping him organize his bosse's library. At a point when I was most frustrated by the people in my room, who I hadn't asked to be there, and who were really bringing me down, I noticed the book on the window ledge and asked that it be handed to me. The artwork on this specific edition is pretty fun and and I was glad that Kailyn had thought to bring it for me. Glad to have that book in that moment, to start back into, to take me outside of that room that didn't feel real, full of beeps and muffled wails from down the hall and the sound of hard frame chairs that skidded across the white floor with an annoyingly loud grating.

"What would you say your pain level is on a scale of one to ten?" The umpteenth interruption of the day. Just as I was becoming enlivened by the spirit of the novel's main character.

"I don't know. 8. But it seems like a pointless question. No matter what number I say, you're going to give me the meds if it's been a sufficient amount of time since the last injection. And if it hasn't been, no matter what number I say, you're not going to give them to me."

"But it's just something we have to ask."
"That's fine but... (sigh) It's an 8. Can I have the dilaudid?"

"No. Sorry, it hasn't been enough time since your last shot."

"But then why ask!"

I didn't care if I got the shot or not. Like Ang said, bone pain is bone pain. But being stuck in a room, stuck in a bed, occasionally questioning whether or not you're alive or dead, if this is some kind of poorly (or perfectly) designed purgatory or a dream being manufactured in a coma or still under the curtain of anesthesia, when these are the things in your life, it feels necessary for common sense to exist, vital that an explanation be understood and counted as meaningful. But these things, common sense, understanding, they seem to have no place in hospitals, or in the vocabulary of this specific hospital where people go about their scripted business, unable to react based on the dictates of the situation.

As the nurse wheeled the ungainly machine out of the room I forced myself to take the situation less seriously. Stepped back into the world of Merricat and Constance and Uncle Julian. A world that was similar to the one I found myself in: cutoff from the outside, beset by uninvited foes. It seems crazy that I've never heard of Shirley Jackson, I thought. A knock at the door. tap tap. "I'm here to take your vitals." Blood pressure cuff, finger clamp thing, crazy paper- thin disposable thermometer. "On a scale of one to ten, how's your pain?"

"It's a ten, but I can't have a shot right now so, whatever."
"OK. I tell your nurse."
"OK. Thanks." I tried to put all the good emotions I could into the thanks, realizing that this woman wasn't at fault. Wasn't even a nurse. Was genuinely just trying to do her job. Not that the nurses weren't... ugh. It's a lose, lose. I would have to try to be nicer to everyone. Even though I thought I was doing pretty damn good, under the circumstances.

I guess it was on Friday, after the surgery, later in the evening, when they told me that I'd be in the hospital until Monday. This was not news I was expecting or that I was happy to hear. Then, today, Sunday, when the physical therapist finally showed, crutches in tow, after he poked and pushed and pet and coached me around the wing and up one set of stairs on those slippery aluminum rods, I asked him how long before I'd be able to put any pressure on the foot, he told me eight to ten weeks, and suddenly, what was originally a lunch date with my girlfriend had turned into two-plus months of bullshit.

That was about four hours ago. People have come and gone since then. Yesterday, I tried to make it absolutely clear that no one was to come visit me for the duration of my stay. I have things that I need to do, I told them. Everyone was very polite and said they understood but I did detect a certain amount of feelings-hurt-type energy. Kailyn spent the night because I wanted her to. Wanted us to have that little bit of time alone, to relax. So after a pasta dinner with her and her mom and my parents, which had been ordered and picked up by her mom from Little Toni's in the Valley, after the order, which they'd mostly gotten wrong, after everyone complained and complained about the food and the wait and this and that, at the point when I thought I was gonna lose my god damn mind for everyone else's constant bitching, there seemed to be a moment of universal understanding where the parents said their goodbyes and left.

"Not a moment too soon," I told Kailyn. I was almost shaking. I cried a few tears made of pure frustration. "No one gets to come in here and complain. No one gets to talk about how shitty their dinner is or that they had this problem or that problem. I got hit by a fucking car! So until I get out of here I get to complain, which I'm trying not to do too much, but nobody else does. I know that might not be fair, but all I've heard since I got in here is about everybody else's problems and my parents bickering with me or each other and it's really all fucking bringing me down. I'm sorry but I just can't deal with it anymore."

"Okay. Okay, babe. I'm sorry," she said. Because she's a god damn angel. And I felt bad for feeling that way about her and her mom and my parents, but it also felt good to have been able to say it. Then we just sat for a while holding hands. I looked at her hand in mine, at her face and hair, I thought about how she had to go to work and how I wouldn't be working for an indefinite period of time. How we lived together now and there were still things to be done around the house, things to finalize our move-in. I called for the nurse by pushing the little button shaped like a nurse on the bed and asked for some pain meds, which they gave me, and then we took out my computer and put on Steven King's *Dreamcatcher*, watching with some amount of enjoyment until she feel asleep on the crappy chair-to-bed-transformer that a nurse had brought in from the hallway or somewhere.

This morning we woke up together. Not in bed at our new apartment, comfortable and excited by the fact of our new surroundings, our shared space— but on separate, uncomfortable beds in this sad, crummy room. I don't think it made either of us sad though. Quite the opposite, even. Without saying so, I think we both realized how lucky we are that tomorrow, (assuming this is not a fever dream or I'm not dead), we will be back in that new apartment, together and stronger for the experience we've had.

She went downstairs and got us coffee, and when she came back up we finished *Dreamcatcher* and spent a little while laughing about things and planning what needs to be done when I get out of here. Then she left. I met with the physical therapist, the orthopedic doctors stopped by to re-dress the ankle and tell me I'd for sure be discharged tomorrow, and I sat in what by now has become this utterly filthy bed, in clothes that smelled, finishing the last pages of *We Have Always Lived in the Castle*, which was really just super enjoyable.

After a day of mostly being left alone, it's ten pm and I realize that, dream or dead, reality or whatever, maybe everything is exactly as it should be. These events may have transpired in exactly the way they were supposed to. I *am* a different person. I will live in a new apartment. I will have nothing that I have to do (other than deal with this healing process) for the first time in a long time. So this is the most complete, the most full-on fresh start that I've had in a long ass time. This is a time for excitement. I will create, love, and let abundance floweth over from my cup, because these are not trials, they are the things that life is made of and I am made to make something of them.

tap, tap. The door opens slowly as a nurse tries to maneuver the cart into the room. "On a scale of one to ten, what would you say your pain level is?"

Him, Her & (Cact)i

How I pity them. I am a cactus. The most sentient of beings. Performing my task to the utmost. At being a cactus, I am perfect. Other things surround me, but they can't do what I do. They don't know that I'm always standing, never have they once heard me complain. Nor have they offered me a chair. Each day I provide them with everything I have, all my cacti properties. They hardly notice. But then, they don't notice much.

Even when, moving close to the window, so that I'm looking down on the cowlick part of his hair, the pinnacle of him, he's staring out at the city, I know he can't see it. Can't see that body tucked back in the shade, the little yellow flowers that have erupted between the gap where the cinder block wall meets the fence slats, or the new teal paint staining the asphalt in the empty shape of a dresser. He can't see these things, and she doesn't bother to look. That's the difference between them.

She can see what she wants, but it's not out there. She doesn't think it is for him either, and lately they've talked about that. I've held my peace. Nothing I can say would help and anyway, I suppose it's not really my place to intrude. She sees a future for them. Together. Doing whatever. It doesn't matter. She wants them to have the things they want, to do the things they want to do. Thinking that, maybe in South America, Holland, even Denver, they could find something in that change of landscape that would bend to their will.

It doesn't take much to keep me alive. A few spritzes of water once a week, a window that receives a moderate amount of sun to exist in. That's how I grew into such an impressive specimen, by not needing much and making the most of what I have. Some might argue that my placement in the sun, the amount of water I receive— these are things that are beyond my control. If they were taken from me, what would I do then?

It's not an absurd line of question, however!— I put it to you: why should I focus on the what ifs that don't apply to me. Why posit a scenario where I am worse off than I am? To plan for the future you might say. And what future should I plan for? I would answer. Which of the infinite number of futures that rely on fractions of a tenth of change to create endlessly different outcomes? Then I would remind you that I am a cactus, perfect at what I do, a well of experience.

So they talk about moving, because it's easier than talking about staying. For her at least. Even moving down the street, that would be a start. *What if we sold everything, bought a little trailer, a really little one, just big enough to sleep in, and we could figure out how to hook it up to the car*; their car is a sedan without a tow hitch, I look at it through the window as he posits this idea, at the rust spots that are slowly eating through the top, have already devoured the clear coat, the paint, and are making a go at the metal— *and we could drive around to all the festivals, like Outside Lands, SXSW, Coachella, there's probably a million more— so we could drive to each one and like, sell stuff.*

What would you sell? I wonder, just as she asks. (We are more pragmatic than he is). *I don't know. You make your jewelry and you could teach me. So we could do that. And then, when we wanted a break we could head up to NorCal and work as bud tenders. I don't know. It was just a thought.* The problem is he's always coming up with thoughts. Like when he applied to Musicians Institute last year, thinking that he could get a student loan and, once he was in the program, with all those tools at his fingertips, he'd be able to record an album for free, using musicians from the school, and then drop out and shop the album to record labels. They went to the orientation one Saturday where he quickly realized that was less of a plan and more of a pipe dream.

But we've stuck with him, her and I. It's not like he's holding her back. She has two degrees, and half of the credits for her Masters. Each time she goes back to school, sure that this new direction will be more to her liking, she winds up back where she started but with more debt and one more thing on the list of stuff she's for sure not interested in. Right now she's working as a dispatcher for a tow truck company, which he hates because he thinks it's bad karma, to which her response is that, until he gets a job, it's what keeps them in weed and rent money.

It wasn't always like this. When I first moved in, 4 years ago this summer, they were living high on the hog from his recent real estate successes. In one year, that year, his first as a licensed agent, he'd made half a million dollars in commissions. He insisted they buy a house, she insisted they stay in this apartment. She got her way, due mostly to the fact that he figured it didn't matter. He was sure, and didn't hesitate to tell anyone who would listen, that this was only the beginning. That he was done working odd jobs and that his lady would never have to work again.

So that's what they did. They were pretty frugal at first, but with her not working, two new cars, paying off all their debt and her starting school again, they were pretty much tapped out by the end of the second year. And he hadn't sold anymore houses. Wasn't even in real estate anymore.

It can probably all be traced back to the weekend they went on their first peyote retreat down in Mexico. I stayed here to look after the place, but when they got home, two days early and still trippin' a little, everything changed. He took a week off work. Then another. And another. By the fourth week he didn't bother calling them at all. At some point they must have talked about it. When I wasn't around. Surely she would've asked him what his plan was. What their plan was. But she was different too.

That's when she started making the jewelry and selling it on the weekends at the Larchmont Village Farmers Market. I've always liked her jewelry. She picks good colors, ones that look like they mean something together. Maybe it's her interior design background or, I guess she could have unearthed this skill set on that trip. Opened a door and discovered a hidden world inside her, full of gems and crystals and twisted wires and rope.

I don't know. But they were both different. Not in a bad way. I won't let anyone believe or say that I talked poorly of them. It has never been my intention to be disparaging. In fact, that is a trait you will not find in cacti. Like robots, and the rules put forth by Asimov, we too are governed by a set of principles:

1. Respect for autonomy
2. Nonmaleficence
3. Beneficence
4. Justice

These rules are strict and cannot be deviated from. Who implemented this programing, among cacti, you ask. Who cares, I say. It's tantamount to asking a human why they exist, you'll get a different answer depending on your sample group. Just like you, we have our own interpretations of the hows and whys and whens of our history. Our creationists v. evolutionists.

But that is neither here nor there. I digress and for that I apologize. When I saw you this morning, as I sat out on the curb amongst the other bits and pieces of their life that had been deemed unsuitable for travel, I said to myself, Freddie, that looks like someone you could spend some time with. Someone, and I believe you've proven me right in my assessment, who will listen to the well of information you have to offer. Will learn from the stores of stories you have collected. When you picked me up and brought me into your home, I was ready for you. As ready I think, as you were for me.

Laura

The impact thunder of stricken bowling pins lit the sky with each pop and sizzle of the fireworks sprouting from the back and front yards of houses surrounding her building. Nine p.m. Thursday. June. People had been talking about the start of summer for several weeks and, aside from last weekends swamp fog saturation, they seemed to be right. The line forming at Jorge's Taco Truck across the street was mostly tank tops and those Adidas sandals with the bar across the toes. Evening wear.

Laura stumped out a cigarette, placing it in the path of a wandering stink bug moving waxen under the powerful lights of the parking lot her building shared with a supermarket. The rusty woven lawn chair creaking beneath her as she scratched the fringes of a bug bite. One of the hundred or so bites that had been multiplying, feeding on her dreams. In the apartment there was currently a brown specimen, its body made of two circles, one bigger and one smaller, trapped at the bottom of a water bottle.

Robert from building maintenance has already bombed her small room once, given her tips and a list of supplies to keep the bastards at bay, but whatever short term gains had been made, the problem persisted. She'd found one in the bed a few hours ago, captured it and called Robert to keep him up to date, proud to answer in the affirmative when he asked her if she'd caught it. She tipped the bottle toward the light, examining the bug under the magnifying effect of the last remaining drops of water..

After nearly two weeks here, in Boyle Heights, on the eastern side of the sixth street bridge- now undergoing a painfully slow demolition- she was beginning to feel the psychological effects of the infestation. A sort of PTSD. Any flicker of hair in the wind, every normally erroneous itch became the threatening calling card of some blood sucking invader. Walking around in public slapping at herself, staring at the area of skin in question, breath held, body motionless, looking for the slightest sign of alien activity. Twice, she'd seen tiny black dots exploring her epidermis, but these almost invisible prowling flakes couldn't have been responsible for the huge red welt constellations that covered her.

With the cigarette out, a powerful stench of stagnant, day old, heat lamp special #1-9 Chinese food blew through in drifts from the back door of the little restaurant adjoining the building. Standing, stretching, moving toward the dumpster with the butt, her eyes scanned the ground like an experienced tracker, carefully trying to avoid stepping on any nightcrawlers who might be out, sucking at the concrete. Headed back inside, she took the long way around a pile of feasting roaches, trying to avoid the following eyes of the crouchers and standers in the 99¢ Store parking lot. She'd be halfway up the stairs before the door shuttered like a semi hitting a pothole, and closed. Turning quickly in fear, startled, but careful to hold the railing to keep from falling. She still wasn't used to the idiosyncrasies of her new building. No one had turned on the hallway lights and, moving through the darkness, she watched the stationary lavender LED eyes of the security cameras watching her. Maybe not watching her, but seeing her. And not seeing her even but, bearing witness.

At the door of apartment A, realizing she'd forgotten her keys inside, she tried the handle slowly. Feeling like, with a slow turn, she stood a better chance of finding it unlocked. It worked, but she wasn't sure if she should be relieved or angry for having forgotten to lock it. Flipping a switch near the door, the dim living room light strained to travel the distance of the hallway. Looking at the floor, Laura was reminded of the mopping that was desperately needed. She moved toward the bathroom, disrobing in motion. Scratching forest green nails, lightly, restrained but barely, across her body. Wanting to rip at the flesh of her torso and arms.

Turning on the shower, standing tiptoe on the cold tile, trying to see as much body as possible in the mirror above the huge wash basin. Lifting each breast, each arm to inspect the armpit. They seemed to be attacking the moist areas where flesh met flesh. I should start exercising again, she thought as she pinched a few finger-fulls of stomach pudge before scratching around an especially itchy bump on the mound above her pussy. Pushing her head toward her pelvis, pelvis toward head, pulling the skin up toward her, she tried to tell if it was a bite or an ingrown hair.

The hot water, turned as hot as hot would get, beat at her skin, knees weakened by the overwhelming pleasure of burning, the water pressure and heat getting at the itch in a way that no scratching could. Burn me, boil me alive, let me lay down and prolong the relief of doing the thing that's been needing to be done. But after fifteen or twenty seconds the sensation would die, requiring movement to the not-yet soothed patches, she would turn or bend to mine the new pockets of relief, like a dope fiend licking the bag.

After the shower, squeaking and slipping down the hall, her sandals wet from the water that dripped down her skin. She thought about googling the best way to dry yourself after a shower. Someone must have figured out a way by now. Unless the secret was just to use like six towels. She needed like— a whole body turbie twist. There was something really off-putting about wet sandals. Something about them that, right after getting clean in the shower, made her feel dirty again, almost instantly.

Laura hovered over the bed. She'd left the room in darkness and had been standing for a few minutes, motionless, to give the bugs time to get acclimated, back to their business, after the disruption of her entry. Little pools gathered at her feet, the towel cinched above her breasts was pinching the skin, but she did not waiver. Thumbing the flashlight on her phone, she began the search for any unsuspecting visitors. In corners and ruffles of fabric, pillow cases and seams, between the wall and the boxspring. But she saw nothing. A couple of dark flecks here and there but, they didn't move, and when she picked them up, they turned out to be bits of lint, tiny threads, etc. As she climbed into bed, doing her best to forget the fact that she may or may not be cohabiting with an unwelcome species, she tried to find strength in the fact that people live with all sorts of bugs in all sorts of conditions. She'd heard that Oprah's best friend as a kid was a cockroach.

!Hay, la ranya (larania?)! La ranya, larania, la raña.

A child's laughter echo's between the wide-smile-sounding words of an old man's playful taunts. In the front or back seat of a car, doors wide for ventilation. This is how Laura pictured them. The old man lifting the little girl, or contorting himself, grandpa entertaining the child while her parents waited in the interminable lines at the 99¢ Store.

She was listening to the scene unfold like a radio drama, her back to the parking lot where they acted out the play. Shoulder blades rested against the fence, the bars hugging the flesh around her spine. La Ranya? Larania? Laura couldn't decipher the the word or its Spanish root. Or was the old man just repeating the child's name? Playing with the phrasing or tones of a word that she understood, able to entertain her without fantastical constructs. Will this be a moment that sticks with la Raña through the years, that is recalled by the grandfather on his death bed? Will Laura, years from now, sitting in a car with her daughter or granddaughter, remember the timbre of that old mans laugh, the cries of delight from the girl?

She was tempted to turn, to see them. Knowing she needed not to. Afraid of interrupting. That might change things. Steal their meaning. Taint the experience itself and her voyeurism of it. Her phone vibrated the flat intermittent pulse of a call through her right butt cheek as she extinguished a cigarette on her shoe. She decided not to answer. Wanting to continue living in the world of la Rania's laughter. When the phone signaled impatience with its short-burst text vibration, she remembered that she wouldn't be able to go back in her apartment all day, towels packed beneath the doors to keep the poison inside where it could kill the most bugs. She was in need of something to do or somewhere to chill.

The car was on, cold air drooling through the vents, she took the phone out, opening Instagram and scrolling the latest posts, checking likes and comments, before remembering why she'd gotten in the car and taken out the phone in the first place.

The call and text were from her friend Dot. Dot who she was pretty close with, well, really close with in a lot of ways, but in a lot of other ways she felt like she didn't know at all. At any given time she wasn't really sure of what Dot was up to, unless they were together, at which time Laura could never be sure of what she was thinking, or, if Dot said she was headed off to do something or meet someone, Laura never knew if what she'd been told was true or a meaningless lie. She didn't care what kinds of things Dot did or who she did them with, but she'd caught her in lies, accidentally, on several occasions, Dot looking sheepish, offering up a thousand excuses.

Laura always wondered if Dot needed to create these convoluted deceptions of no relevance to anyone, in order to make herself believe her life was more interesting than it was, or make other people believe that. But mostly, the lies weren't even interesting or outlandish.

> Dot: You free this week?
> Laura: Yeah, wats up?
> Dot: Just got tix to visit steven in ny.
> Could you watch my place? pls
> Laura: How long?
> Dot: 3
> Dot: Days
> Laura: Sure. When?
> Dot: Be ehre by 2?
> Dot: *here

Laura spent fifteen minutes looking for parking around Dot's building but ended up in a one hour spot, hoping that Dot would be driving herself to LAX so Laura could move into the driveway where she'd be immune from street sweeping and other ticketable offenses. As she walked around the corner, she could see the luggage handles sticking up in the back seat of Dot's VW, whispering a *yes!* to herself as Dot came down the driveway, one last bag wheeling spasmodically behind her.

"Hey girl."

"Hey girl. Thanks for doing this."

"Of course. No problem. What time's your flight?"

"Shit. Like three, I think. I don't even know if I'm gonna make it. We were talking about me going to visit and then I guess Steven found a ticket on kayak or somewhere last night for a hundred bucks or something ridiculous so he just bought it and I've been freaking out all morning trying to figure out who I could get to watch the cats and trying to pack and stuff. Seriously, I really appreciate it."

"Wow, that's cheap. I almost wish I'd gotten one. I really need to start looking for deals and, you know, just trying to travel more. I'm sure you have plenty of time. It's a weekday, there shouldn't be too much traffic. Are you excited?" Steven was Dot's long distance boyfriend and they hadn't seen each other in at least a few months. Laura always kind of got the vibe that both of them were probably not really abstaining if the chance to sleep with other people presented itself, but maybe that's how their relationship had lasted as long as it had. They'd been together for a few years and Steven had been living in New York off and on almost that whole time.

"Yeah, it should be good. I just hope the weather's bearable. Last time I was out there it was just like, so sticky the whole time."

"The worst. So, how many times a day do I feed the cats? And like, what other stuff do I need to know as far as, whatever else?" Laura remembered about the car. "And will I be able to park here or what should I do about parking?"

"You can park here. That's totally cool. And as far as the cats and stuff, I wrote everything out on a piece of paper that I stuck to the fridge. If you have any questions you can call me, obvi, but there's really not that much to do. Help yourself to anything in the kitchen, there's lean cuisines and frozen pizzas in the fridge and I left 40 bucks on the counter in case you need like cat food or liter or something but there should be plenty of all that so..."

"Ok. Well you should probably get going or you're gonna be late for sure. Drive safe, have fun, tell Steven I say hi. I promise to take good care of the place and the kitties. Do you have something to take for the flight? I might have a weed candy or something in my purse."

Dot was holding out the keys to her, saying she was all good, that she'd be careful driving and flying and would say hi to Steven. They hugged and Laura watched as the VW accelerated down the hill, merging, through the stop sign, into traffic and out of sight. She went inside to drop her bag and say hi to the cats, saw the note Dot had left: bold curvy lines in red felt tip with feeding instructions and little jokes, written in the first person feline on "Hogwarts" stationary. The cats were nowhere to be seen, but she figured they'd come out when it cooled down some.

Making sure to close the door tightly behind her, these being indoor cats and Laura not wanting to blow it on the first day, she lit a cigarette and started off toward her car. She walked slowly, along the narrow streets of white, yellow, red and blue stucco, the apartments in a sort of adobe style or at least, showing some adobe influence. She walked past the Music Box Steps, Laurel & Hardy Park and Los Globos. When she got to her car, she was embarrassed to realize she been lightly scratching at underboob for the entire walk.

Dot's cats better not have fleas. She hadn't even thought of that until just now. She'd been so sure this would be three days rest, but now she couldn't keep from worrying that potentially, her place was bug free, and the one she'd just volunteered her time in, could be a breeding ground. Think positive, Laura told herself, pulling onto Sunset and hanging a quick left on Vendome. She parked in the driveway, sitting on the hood of her car and lighting a cigarette. She text Dot about fleas and was assured that both cats were regularly attended too and were certified bug-less.

It was still pretty early but already she felt exhausted. I *have* been up since five, she thought, feeling justified as she unpacked an overnight bag on the kitchen table, slipping in to a pair of pjs and a tank top. She should be looking for jobs but, catching herself picking at the scab of one of the older bites, decided to save that for the following day and spend the few short hours before she passed out watching something on tv. Checking on the cat's food and water, satisfied there was enough to last them through a long night, she stretched out on the sofa, found a channel that was playing seventies game shows and their commercials, and floated in the hallucinatory zone between waking and sleeping for the next several hours.

She woke up sweaty, in something like darkness. Like dusk sort of, but the sky is darker than day and lighter than night and, because you missed a chunk of time that you'd usually be up for, there's an eerie sense of stillness about everything and a loneliness that makes even the inanimate objects feel as though they've turned against you. Laura flipped on a couple lights, kitchen and living room, which almost immediately made the apartment more tolerable, warmer in every way.

A cup of tea or coffee would be nice. Something hot and caffeinated in which to lose her blues. But bed sounded nicer. Brushing her teeth and fumbling through the medicine cabinet, she found a box of Benadryl, taking two and sitting on the edge of Dot's king sized bed, she began applying cortisone cream to any of the bites she could reach, whether they itched currently or not. By keeping the amount of cream light and rubbing it in vigorously, she hoped to prevent ruining the bed sheets with her splotchy residue.

ch   ch   ch   chchchchc   ch   ch   ch   ch
chchchchchchchchchc......thump! chchchchch scratch slide

thump!

What the fuck is that? She was gripping the covers up to her chin. Roused by the weirdest fucking sounds from out in the hall. Like someone dragging a stick through sand and gravel or cleaning a barbecue grill, but then also like, fighting with the barbecue. Or maybe it was the sound of furniture being moved? A thief. Someone who noticed that the place had been void of motion, had seen Dot leave and, maybe Laura had forgot to lock the door. Fuck. It could even be more than one person. It wasn't just coming from the hall, but also from the kitchen and living room, near as she could tell. When she first heard it, she thought she might be dreaming, or not hearing anything at all, or that maybe the sound was coming from outside but, as she became more and more sure of her awakened state, the almost terror that was building, in a bedroom that wasn't hers with only a door separating her from a symphony of noises she'd never heard the likes of, Laura knew she had to do something.

"Hello?" It was pathetic but it was a start. "Hello? Who's there?" The noises stopped. Started again. This was even worse than whatever the situation had been before. Now, who or whatever was out there, seemed to be aware of her in here. And undeterred. Fuck. She grabbed Dot's bong from the dresser, it was the heaviest thing she could see in the room, and moved toward the door. She was going to wait until the noise moved past the frame opposite the hinges and fling open the door, using the bong, if need be, to bash whatever she was faced with.

c h   c h   c h   chchchchc   c h   c h   c h   c h chchchchchchchchchc......thump! chchchchch scratch slide thump!... She threw open the door and.... saw nothing.

Then a white cat came flying down the hallway, literally running on the wall, turned into the room, rocketed up and over the bed and back toward her, its paws scratching at the wood floor for brakes as it slid face first into the wall behind her. Then it looked at her crooked and let out a meow that sounded too much like "hello."

"Jesus Christ," she said. Headed out to the living room with the bong, packing a bowl and taking a big rip, sitting down on the couch and exhaling. The cat beside her now, kneading its paws on her sweats. Occasionally getting through the fabric and poking. "Shit!" She tried gently to push it away. Then less gently. Heading back into the bedroom and quickly closing the door. She was hardly back in before the racket recommenced. But at least she knew what it was. What a weird fucking cat.

"...I know I said it would only be three days but like, how long could you stay, theoretically?" Dot sounded tired. Her and Steven had probably been out late for the past couple of nights. She was supposed to be coming back tomorrow but now it sounded like she wanted another few days. If it weren't for the cats, Laura wouldn't have minded, but god, that one cat especially, was so annoying.

"I mean, a few more days would be fine, I guess. I should be looking for a job but I guess I can just do that from here. The cats are fine but, is there any way to calm the white one down at night? He like, really freaks out, a lot. And then he's quiet, I hardly even see him during the day."

"Yeah, it might have to be for longer than a couple of days Laura. I'm in the hospital here and they say they're going to hold me for at least two weeks. If you can't do it, I can try to find someone else. It's not a problem. I'll figure it out."

"You're in the hospital? For what? Are you OK?"

"I'm fine. I was drunk and me and Steven had a fight and everyone's saying I tried to kill myself and him, but I really didn't, I mean, I did, but not like try try, I was just really upset and... It was more of an accident than anything."

"Wait, what? You tried to kill yourself, or him?"

"What they're saying is both. Myself and him. But he's fine, pretty much, and so am I, so I don't know why the fuck they're keeping me here, but my parents are on their way and I hope I'll be out of here soon... They say they're going to keep me for two weeks though."

"Jesus, Dot. What the fuck?"

"I know, I know. Look, could you just stay there until you hear from me again? I'll pay you to do it. Three hundred a week, you can use all my stuff and have people over, there's weed in the top drawer of my dresser, you can use my computer to look for a job. I'll even call my boss and tell him that you're looking for work and see if he can find something for you. Please, Laura?"

"Fuck. Yeah, of course. Of course. Jesus, Dot. Are you OK? I'm sorry, you just really took me by surprise, I don't even think I asked if you're OK. Are you?"

"Yeah. I'm fine. I gotta go. I'll call you or have my parents get in touch or something. Thanks Laura."

"OK. You're welcome. Feel better and.... don't worry. You'll be fine. Everything will be fine."

Laura went to the dresser and found the drawer with the weed, then, not sure about what kind it was or what type of high it had to offer, she decided to stick with her own, for the moment, needing something that was sure to mellow her out. She packed a bowl in the bong and lay back on the couch. Jesus, what the fuck? Dot had always been... compulsive? Out of control? Whatever the right word was, shit, this was the last thing she expected to hear today. It wasn't like it put Laura out really, and with what Dot had offered it was actually (minus the whole suicide attempted murder part) almost a good situation for Laura. But, fuck. She just couldn't wrap her mind around that story being the reality of the situation. And she didn't even know any of the details. It was a plot straight out of a John Hughes movie.

She checked the cat's food and water, put the forty bucks from the counter into her purse and headed out to Pho Cafe. It was nice to be able to drive somewhere close without the fear of losing the only parking spot near the apartment. Driveways were the thing to have. Hashtag blessed, she thought as she pulled into the cramped parking lot, into what looked like the last available space. Then she remembered Dot, and couldn't think of a hashtag for her.

The bug bites had started to heal, but she stayed in the car for a minute, scratching. She really did feel bad for Dot, but she was also glad to be staying closer to Hollywood, at least temporarily. And the apartment was nice, much bigger than the one she rented in Boyle Heights, with a better shower and more modern kitchen. The fact that she'd have money coming in while she looked for a job was also a plus. They hadn't talked about how exactly that money would be delivered and, potentially, Laura should feel bad or have refused the money out of friendship, or a sense of duty toward a person in need, but those cats really were a pain in the ass and Dot had a pretty good job at a Boutique on Melrose.

She was seated pretty quick and ordered the pho thai, chugging most of the ice water and starting in on the beer while she waited for the hot soup. Catching herself scratching at her thigh, she moved the cold bottle there for a second to relieve the itch which, quelled in that location, moved to one arm, then the other, her neck... it was an endless battle.

If that guy called her, and she definitely had her doubts about whether or not he would; would Dot even have time to get in tough with him (her manager)? She would have to, Laura guessed, to let him know the situation, that she wouldn't be able to come to work. So if Dot gave him Laura's info, and he did decide to get in touch with her, what would the job be that he had to offer? She tried not to get her hopes up, but she knew it was a pretty ritzy place, that the employees made good money— Dot had started there as like, a receptionist/cashier, and been moved up to sales pretty quick and, once she was in sales, they had upped her commission percentage a few times in the first year. Maybe Laura could follow a similar path.

And that's where Dot had met Steven. Not that that was an ideal relationship, obviously, but they had had an enviable life from the outside. Maybe Laura would meet someone that she could start a relationship with that was enviable from the outside and inside. Someone with whom murder/ suicide was not on the table. She could save some money, find a nice place in Hollywood with a parking spot, get a newer car, anything that was an upgrade from the clunker she had now, who could say. She could even become like, a celebrity stylist or whatever that job is where you just go in and organize people's houses, make them more Feng Shui. She'd always thought she'd be good at that and, if she could meet people with money, the kind of people who want someone to do things like that for them...

She paid the check and headed back to the apartment. It didn't feel like a job hunting day so she made some coffee, found a container of international delight caramel macchiato creamer in the fridge and settled at the kitchen table, looking through her phone. Within minutes, she had forgotten about the coffee, completely absorbed by Groupon, thirty pages in and not having seen one item or event that was of any interest, but it was so easy to just keep scrolling, laughing at unexpected deals you didn't want, expecting something you did to pop up just around the next bend.

The phone rang, a number from Savanah Georgia according to the caller id, so she let it go to message, knowing she didn't know anyone from Georgia. When, after a minute or two, it showed the little icon that signified a message, she swiped the screen and hit play; "Hi this message is for Laura, my name is Garreth and I'm Dot's manager over at Fred Segal, she gave me your number today and said you might be looking for work..."

Laura looked around the room. The designer couch, the stained glass bar lamps that hung from the ceiling, the vintage euro entertainment center with its clean lines and simple ornamentation; she thought about the parking spot, about a handsome man and organizing a large white closet, so big a sofa could fit comfortably inside. As she hit the call back button and waited for someone to pick up on the other end, she thought about all of these things and, she even almost thought about Dot, but just before she did... "Hello, this is Garreth."

"Hi. My name is Laura..."

As We Dream the Sleep of Dreams

You were mad once. Batshit crazy. For a while. Years even. And each day that goes by un-afflicted means that, statistically, you're that much closer to the madness again. You're still crazy, of course. But in proportionately lesser ways. You watch an insane person (more insane even than you used to be) in a parking lot across the way, struggle to rip a license plate sized piece of cardboard in half. He's having a real hard time and, as an employee of the store pushes a stack of carts toward him, they exchange tirades, neither of them happy about the presence of the other.

What if that's not what's happening at all. It could be that you are background noise in his dream. The dream where he feels week, unable to muster the strength to tear paper, to tame even the most paltry opposition. He is not mad, hardly able to stand, muttering an unintelligible tune or incantation. This man is a doctor.

In his home, his bedroom, were you to look at him right now, by all accounts you would see a body in restful repose. There would be his partner beside him, their arms barely touching, as close together as they can sleep in this heat. The partner, you would be able to tell by his breathing, is having allergies or has started to come down with one of those rare summer colds. It would be obvious though, that he is still sleeping soundly, untroubled, and that he'll be fine in a couple of days.

Down in their kitchen, a mid-range buzz cuts off with a dry crackle from the back of the refrigerator. If you ventured into the living room, the decor you would know to be tasteful, but certainly not your style. Too bland you might think. Overly ostentatious in its simplicity maybe. A comfortable home, all-in-all, so you continue your voyeuristic open house. Each footstep's creak or thud (they have oily rich wood floors, so mostly it's silent going) a trespasser's secret joy.

Back here in the dream nothing much has changed. The doctor has managed to start a tear in the cardboard but it looks like slow going. But no! He's got it! All he needed was a beginning, a nudge of encouragement to bolster his self-esteem. With the two pieces of cardboard now, he moves like an umpire: in the area where parking lot meets sidewalk, legs wide, bent at the waist, knees at 90° angles, using one piece as a brush the other as a scoop, he scrapes and claws at the debris that has accumulated, defiling his little corner of heaven. He works with gusto, the doctor. Knowing that his time is limited and his task needs completing.

The couch is comfortable, you are surprised to notice, or it would be with a little more wear. On the coffee table there are two medical journals that are of no interest to you, a *Town & Country*, *Wired*, the last two issues of *Time*, and a *Popular Mechanics* with an article about how to make your yard prettier and safer with light. It's a very nice coffee table; a huge square at least three-feet wide, of oak stained a light espresso, the top made of four individual panes of glass, beveled at their edges and etched with a flower or fleur de lis pattern. The television is nothing special, but that's just the thing about televisions, they're all pretty much the same. You can exclaim— *Wow! Thats a huge t.v.* or, W*hat good picture quality*, but no one's ever been like: (whistle) *What an aesthetically pleasing design your t.v. has.*

The doctor has taken out a small brush, like the head of a push broom unscrewed from the handle, and is vigorously attending to the corners and crevices of his kingdom. Someone starts to pull into a parking space, the doctor turns quickly, his eyes informing them that that spot is currently unavailable. They oblige. Doctor's orders. He makes his moves precisely. This is not his first rodeo. Unfolding a towel, rolling it up its length as you would a yoga mat for travel, he kneels upon it and, with a flat head screw driver, starts in on the hardest part: cleaning between the grooves where the curb butts against the sidewalk. With archaeological care he shovels out the day's buildup, always surprised by the amount of sediment that is collected between his nocturnal cleanings.

If you follow the hallway opposite the kitchen, you will come first to a doorway on your right, the office of the doctor's partner, a computer tech by day, which you could easily tell by the amount of screens and hard drives and blinking lights, but what would be harder to tell, maybe (or maybe you're the tech-savy type), what even the doctor doesn't know, is that he is also a hacker of medium grade. He has been trying to code his way into the ranks of Anonymous, for years. His latest project (one for which Anonymous will continue to ignore him) is an algorithm that, once uploaded, will superimpose the face of Guy Fieri on every person, on every frame of every show on every channel, for a twenty-four hour period. A Guy Fieri takeover of epic proportions. Your only real hint to this dastardly scheme will be the bouncing ball screen saver of Fieri's face, his bleach-blonde spikes and goateed smile that adorns each of the office's six monitors.

The doctor has finished with the cracks. With his cardboard and brush he neatens the area, his final touches, and places his tools back in their respective places in his cart. Taking up a blue, two-gallon bucket, he moves among the three trashcans along the perimeter of the parking lot, sorting out the recyclable material, dropping each can or bottle into the bucket, which is quickly filled and refilled. Then, making sure that all of his belongs are secured, that he's left nothing behind, no rock unturned, he surveys his work, pleased at yet another job well done, before pushing off with the cart, toward a new dawn of a new day, breakfast on the horizon.

Further down the same hall, past a bathroom of lovely black marble and copper fixtures, you'll find the doctor's study. Which is why you're here in the first place. You notice the heavy and intricately designed knob on the door, the keyhole at its center. The door is locked, but opens for you. Without having ever been in a doctor's private study, but having seen them in movies and on t.v., it's basically just what you would expect. There are books, what looks to be an expensive desk, imported perhaps, and probably a real bitch to move (you imagine the doctor hired movers for most of the larger items in the house). On the desk are gold pens with the initials of the doctor carved in a tasteful script, a letter opener, blah blah blah. All the stuff from fancy offices.

But it's the bookshelf that catches your eye. The bottom row, right behind the doctor's chair, against the wall at the back of the shelf, behind a set of pristine first editions, you notice what look like the ragged covers of years-old spiral notebooks. You, rightfully for your part, assume them to be the college notebooks of the doctor, saved for their nostalgia, the building blocks of that hard-won degree on which the rest of his life had been built. But when you sit down in the comfortable desk chair— spinning around quietly to keep from waking the doctor or the hacker as they sleep above you— and open the first notebook, the second, third, and so on, you find that there is only one line written. Over and over and over again, in the handwriting of a child, small, a thousand words to a page, a hundred pages to a book and at least twenty notebooks you can see:

"If Jerry doesn't clean the house, Jerry doesn't eat. If Jerry doesn't clean the house, Jerry doesn't eat. If Jerry doesn't clean the house, Jerry doesn't eat."

Orbits'

The fridge was full of gatorades, soda, V8, packs of cheese and crackers with the red plastic stick, string cheese, and beer. Johnny Orbits didn't have a license to sell alcohol, but he'd taped a cardboard sign with a note— Must be over 21 w/ valid I.D. Thanks— written in black ballpoint pen to the shelf. He didn't actually card anyone, but it seemed like he should at least keep the facade of law abiding alive. Oh, yeah, and there was one can of spam in there, that he priced at $5 (in six years he'd had no takers, and being a vegetarian himself, that made him a little happy and a little disappointed at the same time).

He had covered the walls in tinfoil that, after the first few years, had begun to come unglued, a little like Johnny himself, hanging off in places, here and there blocking the maze of bare, multi-watt bulbs that he'd constructed to give the joint an industrial feel. Johnny was an industrial, industrious guy, running a business in an industrial plaza. His business was sound suppression. Or rather, he ran a space where you could be as loud as you wanted without fear of any neighbors calling the cops.

Orbits' Studios, located in Anaheim California, was a rent-by-the-hour practice space. Johnny was the proprietor, manager and sole employee. He was a musician himself and, although he looked like a goth: long black hair, day by day getting dreadier, black shirt, black fishnet thing, black jeans, black combat boots— he was a supporter of anything sonic, and his knowledge of music was far reaching. As long as you paid the tab, which was never more than thirty or forty bucks at the end of each session, Johnny was happy to have you there. Sometimes he'd even pop into a room and listen for a bit, offering a compliment at the end of a jam.

We would usually be there on Tuesdays and Thursdays if memory serves. There was always a movie playing on the big rear-projection screen in the lobby. The concrete floors were never swept and the reptile cages gave off that special reptile smell that most people never quite get used to. But Johnny's clientele weren't much for complaining about such things, and we were no exception.

Most nights would start in ones and twos. Cracking a beer in the parking lot and lighting a cig, warming up. People would trickle in and out, carrying equipment or wandering the spray-painted halls, grabbing things from the fridge and waiting in line to pay for them at the small room Johnny used as an office. Sometimes waiting longer if he was trying to ring up a weed sale on the credit card machine that he never seemed to be able to get the hang of.

I always thought of him more as a host than a business owner. It never felt like a place I was afraid to be, uncomfortable is maybe the word I'm looking for. It was more like, a feeling of luck, that we were lucky to be a part of that place. And once you'd been going there for a while, once Johnny knew your name and you had the lay of the land, when you'd spray painted or sharpied your band's name on the the wall, or put up a sticker (those that had merch), then you felt a certain pride. Like you were part of it and it was part of you.

When I think back on it, there's almost a Madonna Inn quality to my memory, but like, if the Madonna Inn were under creative control of a tweaker who had spent his teens submerged in the music of Bauhaus and Skinny Puppy. Each room, although I wouldn't call the furnishings abundant, was furnished and painted in a different way, due probably to the effects of time and Johnny's collectors spirit. There were couches, often times painted as much as the walls, stained with beer and probably a good amount of copulatory fluids, and now that I try to think, I guess the only furnishings in those rooms were the couches.

But on the walls of every room, the halls, bathroom lobby, everywhere were signs of Johnny's artistic endeavors. Most of us thought he lived there and, I don't see why he wouldn't have. It's not like he was raking in the dough. And he always seemed androgynous, asexual, to me. I only say that because, being older now, it seems like the biggest hurdle in living your life that way is finding someone who wants to live that way with you. But also, I just never saw him exhibiting any of those traits. His every interaction bordered on flirtatious and at the same time gave the impression that there was no end game involved. It was just Johnny being Johnny.

The closest thing to a relationship, a partner, that I can remember, was the ten foot white boa constrictor that was always either around his neck or nearby in one of the many glass tanks. Oh, did I not mention in my description of Johnny his penchant for wearing a boa? My apologies. He really loved that snake. I wish I could remember its name; I want to say it was something female, whether the snake was or not I couldn't guess, but I want to say Bella or like, Guinevere or something. I don't know but I just remember how much Sterling hated snakes and how Johnny would dance around with it like fuckin' Axle Rose or whatever and Sterling would yell at him— "I'm not joking Johnny, keep that fucking snake away from me man," and we'd all fall out laughing. But Johnny would just smile and walk back inside. I don't think I ever heard him laugh. You know those kinds of people? Real soft spoken usually. They never laugh, just smile one of those, coy maybe, smiles like they know it's funny, but like they also maybe know more, some deeper secret that all of the laugh-out-loud people are missing out on.

So we went to Orbits' for years. Me and the band I was in with Sterling, Ortiz and Scotty, or with other people in other bands, sometimes just in big random groups to jam and drink. I know there were plenty of times where I did more drinking than musicianing for sure. But that was the kind of place it was. A place where you could be and do whatever you wanted, as long as you were nice and respectful. I don't think I ever saw a fight there, at least nothing that came to blows. It was a punk rock anti-establishment utopia of the kind that had at one time been fairly prevalent in Southern California but, by the early 2000's had been forcibly gutted from the landscape by economics, general trends or both. Just to clarify, it was punk and anti- in the best ways. You could go in there and, if you could stomach the place and the crowd, you could rehearse Christian music or polka, it was an atmosphere for inclusion.

And then, for whatever reason, maybe it was too far away or something opened up closer to where we all lived, but we stopped going there. I know it stayed open, for a while. And probably continued, along with Johnny, in exactly the same ways it always had. Probably we stopped going to Orbits' gradually. I don't ever remember thinking about the place or the man until years later, in Fullerton or Santa Ana, somewhere with the same out-of-the-way industrial layout. I think I thought we were near it, for a second, and then I realized we weren't and I didn't think about it again.

Until one day, someone, Sterling I think, called or sent me an email, or we were hanging out and he showed me the article online, anyway— Someone brought it to my attention that Orbits' had burned down. There had been a fire that raged, engulfed the building, destroyed everything. And in the corner of the article was a picture, with the words formatted around it like they do in editorials, of Johnny

Orbits himself, looking a little more disheveled, a little more bewildered and a little older than I remembered.

The gist of the story was that Johnny had set the fire himself, in an effort to collect the insurance money. They said that the place had been operating at a loss for years and that Johnny was sick of having nothing or of running the place or was worried about the future. It seemed like a lot of speculation. The only hard facts were that he had been convicted of the the crime and sentenced to a period of confinement, and that, when officers had arrived at the scene, they had found a ten foot white boa constrictor in the parking lot. Motionless, transfixed by the flames.

Dallas

They say everything's bigger in Texas. The churches and flags and empty spaces maybe, but to Azer it always looked like a mix of New Jersey and LA. These were his thoughts from the middle bench seat of a yellow checkered shuttle breezing east on Texas State Hwy 114 toward Dallas. Everything looked small actually. Maybe because of the flatness. Having so few things around offered no sense of scale. Trees flicked past in precision marching columns, disinterested in everything but drinking-in the muddy air, sucking the soil, loose and wet from the edge of Hurricane Matthew.

It used to be that he could only smoke on the road. In Dallas, New York, San Fran or Florida. When he was away from his wife and daughter. He'd relished each cigarette then. Their infrequency. And on those excursions, right after leaving the house, he'd stop and buy a pack that would last the whole trip and then some. One after a glass of wine at the hotel bar, maybe a couple in a row, laughing with a compatriot out under the streetlights of an exaggerated night. "Listen," he'd say, "believe me or not, it's true. That's a true story. I told her to get the hell out. Just like that. Then I hopped over the counter and that got her...him..." He was always confusing his hers and hims. After twenty-seven years in this country he still mixed them up. Knowing the right one in his head as his lips formed the shape of the other. It had become an idiosyncrasy at this point to those who knew him, a confusor for those who didn't.

But smoking had become a habit again, and with the flight, even as short as it was, and the time spent waiting in the airport, beyond security where there was no smoking option other than no smoking, he was looking forward to propping himself up next to his bags and burning through one. It was a way of centering himself. He thought he could probably quit smoking if he were allowed to continue with the behaviors of a smoker. If he could excuse himself from life to stand outside for ten minutes, to collect his thoughts while practicing his oral compulsion. He tried not to be too hard on himself for the cigarettes. His cousin was a cancer surgeon and had told him before: "it's always the ones who self-flagellate that end up under the knife." His brother was a prime example of that. Worried about every god damn thing until he dropped dead at 42. Never a puff of anything. And hell, Baraz turned 52 last month, a cancer specialist for 15+ years and he still smoked two packs a day.

After looking around the brown stucco and concrete in the Best Western parking lot, he found a planter filled with more butts than dirt, added to it, and walked through the single sliding glass of the entrance. The cold air inside was a relief at first, but soon became uncomfortable in short sleeves so he rifled through his bags in search of a sweater.

Approaching the counter, sweaterless but tied up in a light, brown and grey striped scarf, he handed over an ID with a very outdated picture and a copy of the online reservation to the front desk clerk. He was a handsome kid in a blue suit with a gold name badge reading Kishan. "Where are you from— Kishan? Is that how you say it?"

"It is."
"So where are you from?"
"Denton."
"Where's that? You live there still? Or here in Dallas?"

Azer pushed at the youngster's wall of indifference. His need for continuous probing, the smalltalk machine inside him steering the ship. What things of interest, of importance, relevance to his stay, could he learn from Kishan from Denton?

"No sir. That's like, a forty, forty-five minute drive. No, I live a few miles from here. Do you have the card that this reservation was booked under?"

Azer was trying simultaneously to respond to a text from his ex-wife/still-business partner and fish the credit card from the jam-packed leather sleeve in his wallet at the same time, finding little success with either until he set down the phone and wrangled the card with both hands. "You're not billing it now, right? Or you are?" He asked the young hands that took the card and swiped it. "No. Not now," reported an obviously annoyed Kishan.

Hitting send and immediately wishing he'd made up something so he didn't have to get back to her again tonight, Azer took back the credit card, absently shoving it into the wallet as he starred at the screen of his phone, rereading his text and hoping she wouldn't reply.

No. I just got here. Checking in then will call them to secure appoint .let you know

She continued to micromanage him, regardless of marital status.

"How..... How do you like Dallas? (Distractedly. A description that is always accurate). I mean, you know, listen, do you know the closest super market, grocery store, is it on McKinney?"

"Probably. That sounds right. Yeah. Just ask someone and they'll tell you." Kishan was tallying figures on his phone's calculator, or pretending to, while Azer traced the 90° angle of the two sofa sections with his pacing. Looking for the number of that client from Ohio his wife had referred to. Worried about the twelve extemporaneous texts he would receive if he asked for the contact info a second time. At a different time, he probably would have tried to explain to Kishan that he'd just asked *him*. That it was his job to know *and* to help guests based on his knowledge. But right now he needed to find that fucking phone number. Which....HAHA! He'd found it and shot them a text with three options for available appointment times the following day.

He'd never wanted to go into the children's clothing business. That had been her, bleeding into him. He was an auto parts trader from early on. Back in Iran, he'd managed a warehouse for his father: refurbishing ball bearings, carburetors, clutch assembly's, anything that would take a grind, shine, or polish. He learned soldering on little computer boards from his uncle, who'd taken a work space along the back wall of the warehouse where his ever more ambitious laboratory grew and evolved. Azer's father couldn't tolerate his son spending time with a brother he thought of as lazy, whimsical even, if his father had known such a word. So he'd kicked uncle Ryed out of the shop as soon as Azer had shown an interest in his "tinkerings". That was just before the revolution.

When he'd first showed up here in the States after fleeing the uprising, Azer worked for three years with no pay. Never even so much as a coffee from his boss. Their agreement had been that this old guy, George, who'd owned this auto parts shop for fifty three years, would teach Azer as much as he knew and, when George felt that the learning period had come to an end, when the lessons from those three lean years had sunk in, the shop would be signed over to Azer and his brother.

It was. His brother landed in '76 and that same year they got their first business license. They'd really felt like up-and-comers. Built it up and out. Expanded from one location in Manhattan to several. And a few on Long Island. He'd loved that business because of what it took to get there. His whole life. Every bit of chance and hard work he could lay his hands on. But things happen. The business had failed, once, twice— By then he had a baby girl and a wife with a plan. Now he had an ex-wife with a plan and that little girl was fifteen, the age he'd been when he packed his shoes with the thirteen hundred american dollars he could come up with and headed to New York.

Thirty odd years later, he had a suitcase packed tight with thirteen-hundred bucks worth of European designed children's clothing samples and a five day schedule of meetings with past and potential buyers, none of whom he liked. Feet up on the table in his funky smelling room at a Best Western off the freeway on the outskirts of downtown Dallas, he flipped through all the channels, once, then again, walked out to the pool where he smoked a cigarette, water filling up the bowls behind his knee caps as his legs dangled in the blue water that swished and pulled against the curly black hair on his shins and calves. Back inside he turned the t.v. off, then on, then off again, throwing the remote across the room to the couch. What the fuck, he though. What the fuck.

He took a shower. Hotel rooms always have plenty of hot water, and quick. So when he'd finished, tripping over and almost stepping in the toilet for how near it was to the shower (and the sink, and everything else in the bathroom), he was no closer to the end of the night. His phone continued to vibrate and glow with missed texts from no one. He'd started referring to her as no one about three months ago. She was someone, but when he was in the company of others and his phone went off, when he checked the screen and ignored it, people would ask— "Who was that? Do you need to take it?" Initially he'd said it was his wife, then his ex-wife, then they'd ask why she was calling, so he'd have to tell them they were still business partners, so he'd started saying it was his business partner, but then they'd want to know what business he was in or if his partner wouldn't get mad about him ignoring so many phone calls, so he'd have to explain that his partner was also his ex. Now he just said no one. Even in his head. He'd thought about changing it in his phone but couldn't be bothered and he worried about what his daughter might think or say if she found out.

Closing the phone in a drawer and making sure he had the room key, before heading past the pool and through the lobby, into and out of a quasi-courtyard with a cut-rate cement fountain that whirred more than babbled, bounding (almost tripping) across the seven or eight lanes of road that separated the hotel from a Denny's. He reached for the door with just a pinky, to keep the rest of his eating fingers clean, but, like in so many places where hot is the usual for temperature, the door was a bitch to pull, forcing him to use all fingers and most of his arm to pry it open. A blast of air to keep the bugs out, the door practically slamming behind him.

"Be right with you," from somewhere unseen. Another Denny's. Exactly like the one in Sacramento where, after the meal as they'd adjourned to their separate cars, almost nonchalantly, his wife had told him that she'd hired an attorney and was filing for divorce. She'd pulled out of the parking lot, leaving him leaning against his car, not surprised exactly but, in a Denny's? They'd been to Paris, to Rome and Berlin. And she dumped him in Sacramento, in the morning, the faint sound of a burnt-out vacuum cleaner gnawing at thin, restaurant carpet around the area where they'd just sat. Through the glass he'd watched the acne-faced junior college student push that thing around the floor plan, less than halfheartedly.

Back in the Dallas Denny's, a human sized, cartoon pancake-man by the register caught his attention and he went for his phone to take a picture, before remembering that he'd left it behind. He liked to take pictures of himself making stupid dad-faces with things and send them to his daughter. He never knew if they made her happy or not, but they did him, so he kept doing it. He was determined to keep doing that kind of stuff. To try to remind her that she was loved. That he thought of her.

When he told the hostess that he'd be fine at the counter, that he only wanted coffee, it was surprising how noticeably she changed from disinterested to disdainful, grabbing the menu back with a thwack of snapping plastic. Hostess gone, the waitress appeared, looking tired but almost successfully faking a continuous smile.

"How ya doin, Sir? My name is Traci and I'd sure be happy to take your order... unless you need more time. Did you not get a menu? Let me get you a menu.... right around here somewhere's...oh shoot, nope, that one's got jam on it, ooop, but I've got a rag so... How you doin' today?"

"Good, Traci. I'm good. And actually, I'll just have a coffee please. How are you?"

"Well, shoot, thanks for askin'. I'm good too." She put the menu in front of him. "I'll give you a little time with that, unless you know what you want?"

"I'll just have a coffee, thanks." Azer had been smiling throughout, but tried to project a sense of calm, over Traci and himself.

"Oh! Sure. You already said. I'm sorry. It's my second day. How'm I doin'? Not so great I guess. But I'm hangin' in there. Only my second day as a server. Ever."

"I think you're doing great." She looked too old to have just started as a waitress. The thought made him sad. Something had happened to upset her life and, just for a second, his smile vanished. Traci set down the coffee, the milk and cream, then busied herself around the little area behind the counter; wiping, pouring, screwing and unscrewing caps, moving rags and napkins and shakers of this and that, an attempt at looking busy or a need to figure out, to put her hands on all the things in the place, experimenting with where they went and why. He thought she looked lost but felt like he should say something to help her spirits.

"Good coffee." It sounded flatter than he'd expected. She looked back over her shoulder, drying her hands on the rag hanging from her apron before realizing it was wet and re-drying them on her pants.

"It oughta be, I made it." wink. "It might be my second day working in a diner, but coffee, I know. Say, where you from anyway?"

"Could I not be from Dallas?

"I didn't say that. You surely *could* be, but this is mainly a passin' through stretch of road, so it stands to reason you're from elsewhere."

"True enough Traci. I'm from LA. But not really passing through. I came to exactly here, where I will stay for five days, at which point I'll turn around and go back."

"No adventure? No exploration? You like music? You should head on over to Deep Ellum — Thursday, Friday and Saturday nights are a good time around there. Plenty to do for cheap." She topped off the coffee and, noticing the hostess had been eyeballing her, excused herself to go check on the only other diners in a corner booth.

He gave it a good thirty seconds before spinning the stool to face that direction. He was curious about her but didn't want to look like he was watching her, or he was bored. He was almost always bored these days which probably accounted for the reason that, if you were watching him, he never stopped moving. Any interaction with Azer, especially dealing with business (which everything was to him), would give you the impression that this was a man who believed that to be moving was to be being productive. In his case it couldn't be further from the truth. His constant, frenetic pace, made him one of the most unproductive people you're liable to encounter.

In the course of slowly swiveling his stool, he noticed for the first time a huge man waiting for take out by the door. Sitting down the man was enormous. Tall, with a belly as perfectly round as a globe and a diameter no less than three feet. He seemed already to have a large bag of food in his possession but now Traci and the hostess were scurrying about trying to determine what had been left out, what had been paid for and what hadn't and for some reason, Traci kept repeating that it was his birthday. Azer wondered what difference that could make. Was he homeless and this was a favor they were doing him? Or maybe at Denny's you get a discount if you show proof that you were born on this day in history. Azer sipped his coffee and marveled at the absolute sphere that was this man's lower torso.

The man moved off to some other part of the restaurant with the hostess, ostensibly to rectify the situation, and Traci came by with a warm up, asking what business brought him to Dallas. She was huffing and puffing still, looking flustered but keeping it together.

"Clothes." Said Azer. "I import clothes and sell them to boutiques across the country. What brings you to waitressing?"

"Well that's interesting. And you get to travel. Well... It doesn't really matter. That's what got me here. We gotta do something, and right now, for me, it's this. But I kinda like it, to tell you the truth. It's different. But everything's different from something so... you gotta like whatcha gotta do."

"Here, here. True words from an evolved mind. We'd be better off if more people thought that way." Azer didn't know if either of them believed what they were saying, but that's what makes for conversation between strangers. He turned his stool again, back to the counter, elbows resting on its edges, just in time to see the family in the corner booth— a father, mother, three daughters, and the youngest child, a son— just in time to see the son put one end of a long french fry in his mouth and the mother, gingerly taking the other end in hers, eating it toward the center until the met in a kiss.

"That's fuckin' weird," he let slip, turning his stool back and hoping they hadn't heard him.

"You think that's weird, you wouldn't believe some of the people that have come through here in the last two days. Some of these people and the things they're happy to do outside of the privacy of their own homes..." Traci, who he hadn't even realized was still standing there, offered.

"Oh yeah? Like what?" Azer was always on the lookout for salacious stories and he hoped that she'd have something juicy for him.

"Well, just this morning..." But the door opened, the fan whirred to life and the hostess was off doing something else. Traci held up a finger that she'd be right back and headed over to greet the new party. "How ya'll doin' this evening?" More and more people crowded through the doorway and Traci looked as though she'd have her hands full for a while. He left a five under the empty coffee cup and gave an unnoticed wave as he headed into the night.

Lighting a cigarette and leaning against a light pole out front, bathing under a light that reminded him of the auto parts shop, he looked around at the strip of hotels and motels. On the other side of the parking lot was a sleazing place advertising itself as a Hawaiian massage parlor. It looked closed, but on closer inspection you would find a small service entrance with a sad blinking OPEN sign. On the other side of that was a hamburger joint claiming to have the best burgers in Texas. Neither place looked like it was on the up and up, both looked like you could walk away with something you hadn't gone looking for.

"You got a light?" It was the big man from earlier, waddling slowly towards him on surprisingly skinny legs.

"Sure. How you doing tonight?" At this point Azer didn't care but he was in a decent mood and offered a smile as he handed over a lighter.

"Me? I'm doin' goooood. Just had three steaks. Perfect. I mean just beautiful man. A t-bone, a sirloin, and what was the other one? Idonknow, but they all three tasted like butter."

"Cooked just right, huh?"

"Like, not too rare and not too medium, wooooo! They was good." He smiled as he handed the lighter back to Azer. "Where you from man?"

"LA"
"Oh so you know how to party. I got coke, weed, speed, dirt, I got that yellow ice..." Azer gave a little chuckle. "No thanks. I need to be up early tomorrow for work, otherwise I'd take you up on it."
"OK man. Well hit me up if you change your mind."

He watched the guy heft himself into a cab, wondering how, without having exchanged phone numbers or any information at all, this ravenous drug dealer expected him to get in touch, but whatever. He almost wished he'd taken the guy up on his offer. Just for a bag of weed or something. But then he'd never make it out of the hotel room. Especially for those first meetings so early in the day. There were gonna be 300 texts on his phone when he got back to the room.

He lit another cigarette and headed down the road toward the 7-Eleven where he could hear a couple of Corona's calling his name.

San Juan

There was uncomplicated but appealing woodwork garnishing the trim, in white semi-spirals, of the old-with-new-paint single story structure in front of me. Sitting there with me, I guess. Or near and large enough to seem close, but not large enough to throw much of a shadow. At the San Juan depot. Just across the tracks. It had been waiting there much longer than I had. Maybe it wasn't waiting. It wasn't and couldn't, go anywhere. Not without a hell of a lot of effort anyway. So it was there, just being itself.

About an hour had past since I hefted myself and my pack from the back seat of that taxi, driven by an older woman who'd decided we would talk about the insurance marketplace and its effect on at-home caregiving as a profession. An hour that was only supposed to be twenty minutes according to the schedule. I don't mind telling you that, until a few short moments ago, after the first twenty minutes, through to about the fifty-eight minute mark, I was busy working myself into a frenzy about my recent bad luck with trains. Drowning in frantic thoughts about everything that should've been happening and wasn't, about what I needed to do when I got back to LA before my lady friend came over. Re-doing the math that had worked out earlier but, now that the train was late, wouldn't give me enough time to do all the things I needed to do. So what things would I do before she got there, what things to save until after we'd gotten settled?

I was sitting with the old house, office, whatever it was, having not yet noticed it. Sitting at the most remote of the shaded tables at the far end of the track. The breeze was that warm, pungent Santa Ana, as dense in its gusts as its per capita content of dust and pollen and almost smokey scent. The sun was hot, the shade only slightly less, a piece of hay, carried across the tracks from the petting zoo next to the house, danced golden through my sight line before catching in my arm hairs. Gently.

I've been listening to Anderson .Paak's *Malibu* and Flying Lotus's *Los Angeles* a lot recently. Both those albums do things that I really like in music. Things I would want to try if I was making tunes. There's a newness and a creativity that draws from a large and varied pool of source material. I think, part of it too, part of what has drawn me to those two albums and albums that I'd put in that sort of category, is that I'm trying to do those same things. Make those sorts of noises with wherever I'm at.

While I sat there, really debating whether or not to abandon my post in search of a cup of coffee to-go, I heard a line in one of .Paak's songs that has really been a grounding note in all of my recent listens. I can never remember what it is, and I'm listening to Zevon now, but basically it struck a chill-the-fuck-out chord and I was released. I noticed the house, tried smelling for the livestock smell in the wind, realized that the scene was not how I'd been picturing it at all.

The train was only a symbol. I can relax at my parents house, where I'd been dog-sitting the last thirty-six hours, but it's been a long time since it felt like home. So the train was my freighter to a better future. Its arrival, a signal of my soon-to-be return to comfort. But I'm never really comfortable at home. There's no couch, only a couple of hard plastic folding chairs and my bed. It's not even a house. Just an apartment I rent a room in. And once I got home, I'd have to do all the things on my list of things to do, i.e. grocery shopping for the week, probably some laundry, then make dinner and lunch for the next few days, etc. I'd had a day and a half to relax at my parent's and I never even got past settling in. When I get home there's things to do. So that period in between was like, a pass. A time to be nowhere doing nothing and I was wishing it away.

At about hour-ten marker, a camera crew showed up. I offered to move but they insisted on working around me. It was interesting, as a person who's into photography, to watch them work, and to wonder about the fifty-something, balding, bespectacled guy they were photographing. What was his deal? I thought he could be a city councilman, or running for a similar type of position. Or maybe something to do with the chamber of commerce, or a local businessman getting a spotlight in the local paper.

He was a hard guy to pinpoint and maybe he even did something cool. I don't like the idea that I'm pigeonholing him as a square but that was the vibe I got at the time. While I was waiting for them to finish so I could smoke a joint, I turned my attention to the photographers. It wasn't clear whether this guy was the one paying them, but whoever it was must have been shelling out a pretty good amount of dough, 'cause there were about six of them; at least three with hand held cameras, a fourth with a tripod mounted video unit and one or two with those large reflective things for lighting. All of the equipment looked expensive, and there was quite a lot of it.

So I was wondering what their deal was, if they worked for a paper, a company, if they were a studio or a for-hire, all-occasions type outfit, did they do their marketing online, who was their client base, how were they getting the word out, did they enjoy what they were doing, did they have other jobs (like working at whole foods or in an office), etc. Basically, seeing people doing something in the neighborhood of what I'd be interested in doing and wondering how they were making it happen.

I was even thinking about asking one of them some of these questions, if the opportunity presented itself. But they took off in another direction, headed to a different locale. That was OK. It wasn't a missed opportunity. I was feeling good. Finally relaxed. Still wishing I had some coffee, but relaxed. Maybe even better off for the lack of coffee. I sparked the joint and a cigarette to mask the smell. There was no movement in the house. All the windows were closed. It was the kind of house that looked like it should never be locked up. But I had the sense that it was, right now at least.

Gathering a pool of spit on my tongue, I tapped the cherry of the joint there several times before putting it away and dragging my cigarette. I knew that area of San Juan had been there for years. Knew that the house was old and thought that maybe I'd even been past it before, close enough to read a plaque or inscription about it being a historic landmark or something. That's one of the things that's weird about being a kid, at least for me, growing up in that place, I was never very interested in the history of it. Always knowing that my destiny lay elsewhere, perhaps. Or never realizing there was a history to it, selfish in thinking that everything existed only for me.

I tried to picture the house, the area, through time. I kept the house looking the same. Even the station and the surrounding buildings on that side of the tracks, being a historic district (I thought), everything would have all looked basically as it did now. Maybe not all the way back to the time of Padre Serra, but a hundred plus years maybe. I removed cars and the roads they were parked on. I made everything dustier. The best way to travel through time is to add dust. I opened the windows and doors of my building. I let the white lace curtains blow and tangle.

On the porch, there was a woman, old (of course. Another good way to travel through time is to make everyone older.), sitting in a rocker in long, heavy skirts, doing something with her hands. It's something small and I was a little too far away to tell what. Two children ran past, the legs of their pants rolled up, bare feet kicking up dust clouds as they chased a chicken through the yard, laughing (not the chicken).

The mission bells tolled and the old woman got up and moved inside. Someone called to the children that it was time for mass. It could have been her, but the voice sounded too young. Minutes later they emerged, not really dressed up but, cleaned, or spit shined maybe. The voice that had called to the chicken chasers may have been that of an older brother. He wasn't a man, but he was old enough that for him to chase an animal, usually meant there was blood to spill.

They headed out; the old woman, the older boy and the two younger, their bare feet now shod in brown leather. Grandma, as I assumed her to be, closing the door behind, heading left at the bottom of the steps, past the stables, the cantina, making a right over the train tracks, through the little ally, warning the boys to watch their step around the manure, instructing the oldest to keep the children under control during the service; she would be helping with the communion and refused to be made a fool of by her grandchildren. She wouldn't have the whole town talking about those rowdy boys of hers. "I tried to instill the same principals in your father," she said, "and look what happened to him. I expect more of you."

My cigarette burned my fingers and I dropped it. The train came with an air horn blast that abolished my daydream. I jumped up and power walked along the platform to make it aboard before the doors closed, knowing the stop would be brief because of how late they were running. I found a seat up top, where I always sit, facing away from the direction of travel and, as the train pulled out, kids yapping, parents paying them no mind, I watched the house as pepper trees and a growing distance, pushed it out of view.

Rice & Tea

Anogachi wears his fathers clothes. The fitted suits bought before the mother and father moved to San Diego. Before the father died. They were the same size. His mother, he, his father, his father's suits. He could probably wear his mother's clothes as well. And she the suits. Sometimes they were old and had to be mended. The suits. And people.

Anogachi has, still has as he looks in the mirror, a slim sharp face and a flat chin. He dreams of what it would be like to make a world of scraps. Pieces of linoleum in different shades and thicknesses woven between patches of rugs and carpet coarse and fine and long. From Rugged planks of redwood hang sheets of metal shelving prominently displaying painted or burned artifacts of cardboard wire mesh and clay. A jacket comprised of 2 blue pant legs sewn on to an orange vest, in the pocket a sundial timepiece made of shells held fast to the pocket by a fine gleaming chain of braided cat whiskers. Lightning fine silks of twisted leather and in the middle of the room a severed water heater sputters flame and smoke while a boy rolls cigarettes made of flac seeds and gun powder. A sharp recycled world full of droning reverberating dripping noises in an oscillating cabinet where a man with arms made of microphone stands batters pieces of meat in a hubcap before searing them on the hood of an old Buick.

Anogachi thinks these things while absently picking at the edge of the wooden counter, watching the vibrating mirror rumble of the puddles and the sounds of feet and cars that trip through them on the streets. Watching the unmoving picture of this building in the reflection of the windows of an across the street one. These are the days of ringing in the ears and thunderous drumming, when little cotton balls drip down the sides of the candles in the window and the steam from the tea is cold when it hits your face. The mail comes with the mailman in his white pith helmet he insists on wearing shorts because he's got to trek it on foot and he thinks the shorts highlight his most attractive quality - the taught hairless golden thighs he's so proud of - the foggy sweat nearly oozes out of him and Anogachi thinks he can see the thousands of tiny broken blowoff valves slowly leaking from too much pressure or a corroded seal.

The mailman always wants to talk Cantonese even though he knows Anogachi has never learned a language but English. Knows he failed the first and only semester of Spanish in high school. The mailman was a classmate for 12 years so he knows this and many other things. He knows what bothers Anogachi, making use of this knowledge. To needle him. Thriving on disharmony and angry greedy lust, a lust for seeing the rage behind people's eyes. Our hero tries to ignore him whenever possible. Thinking that by not falling prey to his pettiness he is doing them both a favor. He would like to learn Cantonese overnight just to prick back at the bastard. This would only make things worse. Perched stoop-top across the way a man is yelling at all passers by "we are the onion people and your downfall is our objective and gain".

Anogachi moves to the door to watch him. In the door of a shop, this shop, which still doesn't feel like his, (he is not contained in the windowed reflection of the adjacent building. Where his body would be stands a thin pillar covered in torn posters and nails,) breathing the fresh cluttered city air, a needed break from the small space at his back crowded with objects defying any cohesive genre, any common thread, save their mostly overall unnecessary existence. This he has in common with his wares. His first days in charge, really in charge, when his father was dead and all his dark suits lined the closet of the apartment above the shop, after a lifetime of wandering the close isles as a peon, sweeping the dust from corners, poking away at the register, standing, father over his shoulder (he feels him here even now), telling him this or that about stock, ordering, merchandising, the needs and wants of the community, for those first few months he had thought of what he could do with the place. What he could turn it in to. But now he is resigned to the facts. That people will buy bug zappers in the summer, umbrellas in the winter, and incense year round. That *Hustler*, black plastic shrink wrap covering the exposed pussy parts, will sell better than *American Art Collector*, and OJ will move only riding shotgun to Vodka.

Stepping from the doorjamb, the electric motion activated bell dings the re-entry of his character.

Scene: A wet day, a mostly-dry lonely shop. Lighting a clear dim. Newspapers soak up water leaking in off the sidewalk. street-junk-dry footprints of the proprietor stain the floor passing a yellow "Wet Floor/Piso Mojado" sign. A hundred packs of dusty old gum on wire racks below the counter. Cigarettes of every color, never dusty, line the space hovering above the register with its keys long worn blank of their numericals, the faint smell of old refrigeration and knick-knacks, scarred flooring where shelves have been dragged in rearrangement, the faded posters of scantily clad in slutty vaguely sports themed women hawking Budweiser/ Coors/ Cuervo hang, the promotional remnants of past super bowls with their roman numerals.

Anogachi takes in hands the book, face down, spine split on the counter, and the stool, moving back over to the door, positioning himself with enough space to let a customer (there will be none today) through. The bell dings to tell him he is back at the door. His only reliable interaction (the batteries have never been replaced as far as he knows, but the computerized tone tolls strong as ever). The book sits open without effort on his knees. The spine broken to submission after so many readings. Lost for a moment again, forgetting the book, unconsciously hypnotized by the saturation out-of-doors. Starting back in on the story he needs not go back a page to remember what is happening. He knows without knowing, just as he did the first time he read it. *The Woolgatherer* by William Mastrosimone. Cliff and Rose. So simply complicated their story. Language of the street. Jersey, but no different than here. Looking up again at the soggy concrete of buildings percolating into soggy concrete canvas of the city's foundations. He is no Cliff (in some ways he wishes he was. The life of Cliff holding the same allure it does for Rose. The promise of a distant and ever changing landscape. The strength of a man persisting past the boundaries of logic and knowing it. Deriving strength from his own strength in the knowledge that he will carry on), but he reads and re-reads, with the hope that his assimilation of the text will somehow coalesce with the weaving patterns of the galaxy to send a Rose to him.

Looking down at the book, a woman walks past his upper periphery. Bare calves sexy, cut, defined, glowing beneath the navy business skirt whipped and accentuated, drawn attention to, a beckoning "look what we have here" with each gust of the tan overcoat that dances from her shoulders fighting the elements. Unknown mystery of the algorithms in his brain make him think of the mailman. Who speaks cantonese and used to call him faggot in high school (though he seems to have forgotten that now).

##*#*

The bare foliage green walls surround him, covered in pictures and hanging things he does not see. Unblocked by invisible decor, exposed behind indiscernible accoutrements. He can see all the things, the ten thousand things, but they are not his. They are remnants of other people's lives. His parents. He does not know what to do with them so they do not exist. He has no desire, no motive or attachment, and so seeing them, they are valueless. In their valuelessness they need not be disposed of. Their location does not affect their value, so they might as well not-exist here, where he doesn't have to see them.

The tea kettle whistles as he remains unmoving at the window. The same view from the shop door below, now higher, now darkness. Still, even in his reflection, he remains out of frame. Moving the kettle off the burner, letting the blue flames lick the grooves of his fingertips, moving them when the burning changes to cold white pain. Examining the persistence of the sensation before it fades. Filling the dented Coleman thermos and throwing in two tea bags before placing it on an invisible credenza and retrieving a jacket from the closet. Moving down the staircase, through the store silhouetted with looming figures painted dark black by the streetlight glow outside. The bell tones, disgruntled by the disturbance, as he struggles with door and the cold metal lock. The thermos waits back in the apartment for him to remember. It doesn't have to wait long.

#*#*#*#

Weaving through the falling Tetris blocks of people, always noticing himself the only traveler in his direction. In the past, switching to the other side of the street, rounding a corner, turning around to swim with the school, but always dodging, always against the grain. So now he moves whichever way, knowing the inevitability of the complicated rushing dance, until he gets to the place that feels calm. The calm is elusive and moving and never in the same place twice. It is looking for him and he must move to help it, must bat away the confusion to leave himself as a lone beacon silently chanting, luring the calm from its scattered hidden places. So some days it finds him quickly, slowly, or not at all. He sits on benches or table tops, bus stops, lunch counters, bar stools, stands at the railing above the bay watching the gulls taunt the water with their smooth aerodynamics, starring at the bridge and its imperceptible movements, feeling the calm searching for him, never sure of the distance, pouring the tea and sipping from the 8 oz. silver cup till it's gone. Returning home, having found or not found his moment.

##*#*

Five years ago he was young and married, poor and unhappy. Now he is young and divorced, rich and unhappy. When his mother died she left him rich. Left him with bills and enough money to pay them. Enough money to pay all the bills he'd ever have and more. Left him the building that contains the store and the apartment, with the affairs of mortgages and estate taxes and the selling of the house in San Diego and a hundred other things he had no previous experience handling. Having no siblings he was forced to deal alone. Dealing was a thing he was long practiced at.

Taking action, not so much. His wife filing for divorce 6 months before, running off, or really, unceremoniously, unflinchingly walking away for the benefits her new man and his money could offer. He was not happy or sad to see her go, but he wondered how it would work out for her, for them both. And then he got the money. Didn't know if she knew that or not, or how she'd feel about it if she did know.

It wasn't until she'd left that he realized how much he identified himself with the comfort that she'd provided. How he'd never really had any dreams of his own. How he thought he'd packed away his childhood and taken on a partner for his problems when he pushed that ring over her knuckle. She would have chastised him for his feelings if she could have seen him then. For the way that he chose to cope with the loss. He was different in a way she couldn't understand. She was different in a way he didn't try to. He thought about the ways she would complain about him when they were fighting. She would start by confronting him in that living room.

Surrounded by the little mimicked tapestries his mother had painted in a community center art class, the bronze plate in its wooden cradle on the credenza feeding off the light from the open window, catching his eye with its golden dented surface as she continued hollering from the kitchen. She told him he wasn't like the other guys she'd been in relationships with, other guys she'd fucked casually. Now from the bedroom, banging drawers and riffling through whatever, part of her acting at busy anger, part of her domineering to make up for his lack of testosterone. Why couldn't he be more regular? She didn't need him to be anything special, but why couldn't he be more like Tracie's husband? Anogatchi wondering if it was too late, if the argument was too far along, to suggest they go get clam chowder bread bowls from the wharf. Tracie's husband played video games involving various types of sports ball and first person online multiplayer team based shooting games. Why couldn't he do that? She talked about how Rob, he guessed that was Tracie's husband's name, had invited him over a dozen times for video game beer days or super bowls, and why couldn't he ever say yes. He wondered why Rob and Bob and Bobby could all be the same name. How Jack could be John. Those Kennedys were a funny bunch. He mentioned something about not realizing he'd been invited to said events. *You wouldn't go anyway,* she retorted from the bathroom. *You've just blocked it out. I know you don't even remember who Tracie is. You're such an asshole. You're not even interested in my friends.* She's right, he nodded to a bird on the window ledge. She wants me to scream at television, to defend her honor in barroom wrestling pits, drunk and glistening with gladiator masculinity, to ride a motorcycle and wear a helmet with one of those faux mohawks jutting green broom wisp out the top. The bird cowered, head beneath its wing at the thought and flew off.

He would promise to go to the next social event one of Tracie's friends boyfriend/ husbands invited him to. He would promise to hole up all day in some sad "man cave" drinking pilsner that was much too cold and exchanging plastic controllers warm and soggy from serious game play. He would promise her all these things so he could get his clam chowder bread bowl. He would mean it too. And then the day would come and he'd think up some excuse, something about the store or errands, or he'd show up just long enough to say he'd gone, eat some gourmet chips from a bowl on the table, watch a few games of *Madden* or *Call of Duty*, then use one of the excuses he'd formulated on the way over, and make his exit.

He wasn't glad she was gone, but he was a little glad she wasn't here anymore. She seemed to suck the air out of rooms with her blustering, Anogatchi watching the walls bow in, convex in the vacuum she created. She had been right. He hadn't put much into the relationship. They both seemed to want someone else. He couldn't even remember now how they'd been in the beginning. Couldn't remember a time when it wasn't like that. He had done things for her. As she had for him. Unfortunately they had all been things they thought the other wanted or needed, without really taking that person into consideration at all. They did things for each other that they wanted done for themselves. She would take him to the newest trendy health food joints, where he would laugh about the tonics and elixirs. The grains of salt, hand picked granule by granule from distant ports of call, a sprig of cilantro on a slice of lemon, $7 olives. Snake oil hawkers through the ages have done just the same he'd say. So she would get mad. And when he dragged her along to Stater Bros. or Smart & Final, or to that store where you could buy a deli slicer and one of those huge coffee pots for business meetings, she would stomp around in protest, make comments about the class of people there.

Then there was the money. She made a good amount. Or what he thought was a good amount, and she thought wasn't nearly enough. Which, since he made far less with the shop, meant that he made less than not nearly enough for her tastes. They had the apartment and the store because of him. Both of these she hated. But really, he did too. So he didn't bring much to the fray. And after his folks got sick he was spending more time away from the green apartment. More time in San Diego watching them die. And since he was watching them die instead of watching the store, he brought in even less money, and the longer he was away the more she thought about how nice it was that he wasn't there. So he understood why she left. He may have even found a way to get her to leave without facing the conflict of it.

&&*&*&*&*&*&*

After the wife left, he'd spent the last six months of his mother's life with her down in San Diego. The little father was dead and buried, and the mother was next. So he locked up the shop, unplugged everything in the apartment and sealed the windows, put a mail forwarding form in the hands of the nemesis postman and drove down the coast with a bag full of clothes. When he arrived, he gave the hired nurses, a man and woman who switched off nights and days, the week off, telling them he'd be there indefinitely, that they'd get a paid weeks vacation, and when they returned, he'd be there to help out and hang around.

He sat with his mother. Listening to her memories. Asking her about the things from her past that existed for her before him. She was stuck back there. But sometimes, for no reason and for the first time in his life, she seemed to see him clearly. To know him, or something in him, better, clearer than he could see himself. Then zipping back to the past. Asking him if he remembered things from before she'd met the father. From when she was a little girl. Reminding him of things he'd never known about people he'd never met. And for some reason, in that week, alone with that person he could never say he'd met before, he seemed to see something too. He saw a proud, multi-faceted human. A scared child. A strong fighter. A beautiful woman lost in the inevitable decay, all hands on deck throwing all the switches on coping mechanisms, a foggy radio communication to the outside world. But he saw her and felt that she was real. This was all real. It was all too much to deal with. In that week he cried. In that week he laughed. One morning after being up all night, they slept. Peacefully, in the matching recliners, Anogatchi where the father would have been.

That afternoon he started going through the house. Looking for things to keep occupied in the downtime. Opening the top of the old chest at the foot of the bed. Leafing through the trinkets and treasures he had never seen, neatly packed below the dusty linens. He helped her paint her nails a boisterous red. The room taken over with the chemical smell of the polish, the remover, all the glass and plastic bottles, the cotton balls and q-tips, perfumes and powders that lined the counter. He rouged her cheeks at her request. Laughed at her complaints of his technique. I've never done a woman's makeup before Mom, he explained. But you've seen a woman, she was looking at herself in the mirror, and a woman doesn't look like that, pointing to her face. He noticed a picture of the father and her, so young, vibrating faded photo beaming with youth. Bouncing curled hair she, the father pre-bald.

In a closet at the far side of a long, thin room, he found the mountain of books. Books of all sorts. Books thin, fat, square, paperback, magazine, first edition, reference, in German French Italian Japanese Greek. Some jammed full of notes, papers, photos, some with spines never dented, pages with gilded edges stuck together since the day they were printed. *What's with all the books?*, he called out, forgetting she was sleeping. He pulled from the outermost stack, the only pile that seemed it wouldn't Jenga down upon him.

"Except for shoulder yokes carried by the men, baskets were almost the sole transport for everything not liquid. Women wore a head ring on which they placed large jar baskets or shallow trays. In the containers they carried almost everything including wood, plant harvests, meat, and washing. Baskets were used for winnowing and storage. They served as suitcases, sand buckets, and refuse pails." From a small 16 page pamphlet published in 1970 - *The Seri Indians of Sonora Mexico* by Bernice Johnston. He googled winnowing:

'winō/
verb
gerund or present participle: winnowing

1 1.

blow a current of air through (grain) in order to remove the chaff.

> • **remove (chaff) from grain.** "women winnow the chaff from piles of unhusked rice"

> • *synonyms: separate (out), **divide**, **segregate**, sort out, sift out, filter out; **More** isolate, narrow down; **remove**, get rid of* "the chaff is winnowed from the grain"

> • **remove (people or things) from a group until only the best ones are left.** "the contenders had been winnowed to five"

> • **find or identify (a valuable or useful part of something).** "amidst this welter of confusing signals, it's difficult to winnow out the truth"

> ▪ *synonyms: separate (out),* **divide**, **segregate**, *sort out, sift out, filter out;* **More** *isolate, narrow down;* **remove**, *get rid of*
>
> *"the chaff is winnowed from the grain"*

"Obstructions and dangers in the water are also charted, and symbols tell the mariner what to be ready for. It is worth bearing in mind that a wreck, even one that's largely exposed, soon ceases to look much like the ship it once was, and may be difficult to recognize." There are two radio channel guides from the Federal Communications Commission marking this page of the Ninth Edition, Fourth Print of *Boating Skills & Seamanship*. There is a United States Coast Guard Auxiliary Certificate of Completion in the Boating Skills and Seamanship Course with his father and mother's name in typewriter and signed in ink by the Flotilla Commander.

"A historic sequence of photos taken by Eadweard Maybridge in 1878 at the behest of Leland Stanford settled a $25,000 wager that a galloping horse would at some time have all four hoofs off the ground. With a set of twenty-four cameras tripped by wires, the photographer proved Stanford right and contributed to the early development of the movies." Paul C. Johnson's *Pictorial History of California* published in MCMLXX, which, looking up online, he found to mean 1970. The book bragged of having more than 275 illustrations which, it didn't seem like illustrations were necessarily the most accurate way to portray history.

He found a version of the Qur'an. The "International Bestseller" printed at the top, almost as big as the title. (Line 123) "Thus we have placed leaders in every town, its wicked men, to plot (and burrow) therein: but they only plot against their own souls, and they perceive it not."

Over the course of that week he worked through the nights. Attending to his mother and to the stacks of books with almost equal care. Soon the room was filled with small piles, arranged in loose genres, enough room between the rows to sit and move. On the seventh day, the day before the caretakers were scheduled to return, Anogatchi sat in front of the pile made for religious texts. The smallest group in the room. He was flipping through the pages of a large book, the pages alternating English text on the right, and on the left, the deft black Chinese brush strokes, with their vertical columns right to left. The 81 meditations of the *Tao Te Ching* by Lao Tsu.

"Eleven:

Thirty spokes share the wheel's hub;
It is the center hole that makes it useful.
Shape clay into a vessel;
It is the space within that makes it useful.
Cut doors and windows for a room;
It is the holes which make it useful.
Therefore profit comes from what is there;
Usefulness from what is not there."

&&*&*&*&*&*

Those six months were spent in watching the decline. Playing good cop when his mother had decided the nurses were the enemy. Pushing her, bundled wool in the wheelchair, up and down the same cul-de-sac, a different street in her eyes each time. The day when the paramedics and doctor and nurses stood around her rigid frame imperceptibly shading to blue, propped at a hundred-and-something degree angle against the ever-present mountain of pillows on the bed. In the following days and weeks and months, Anogatchi talking with lawyers about executing the estate, with real estate brokers about repairs and escrow windows, with morticians about funeral options, casket upgrades, about the advantages of burning a body. Then he was back home. In the parents apartment above the parents shop that he reopened on days when he felt like it.

At that time he slowly began to realize he was free from all the attachments of a previous life. There was almost no one left who could prove he'd ever been anything. No one to hinder him with you never used tos or I wish you wouldn'ts. He started going out more. Spending some of the money he found scaling the walls of his bank account. He tried gambling, expensive women, bought a car, went on a helicopter ride, took a week long trip to NY, spent a month in South America. He grew his hair long, shaved it off, tried wearing hats, bought a watch then gave it to a neighbor. Then he let himself back into the shop, propping open the door, and settling back into the routine as it'd always been. It could have been years or days or months since then. This familiar world swirling around unchanging, a Bill Murray *Groundhog Day* type sitch. Losing the days in the knowing exactly what comes next. He found himself no closer to anything, and not nearly as far away from some things as he'd thought.

&&*&*&*&*&*&*

Five years had passed when he discovered the books again. He had bought the new car four years ago and had never gotten rid of the old one. He found a charity that accepted donated cars for shuttling around the blind and was up to his elbows cleaning out all the junk and collected detritus that had been aging in the statue né car. He carried the deteriorating box from the trunk into the shop, lifting it up to the height of the counter, one corroded corner giving way and all the books sliding out in a waterfall of paper and dust to the floor. That's when he found the Mastrosimone and the Tao Te Ching.

The car was gone and in the empty spot, surrounded by a short wall of brownish weeds the exact shape of a sedan, he placed a round white table and a collapsable camping chair. He spent the early hours of the day and the late hours of the night here. Reading the two books, almost interchangeably. That's when the calm began. It was easy at first, to find it there. With time continuing to pass, the weeds creeping closer in, losing the definite shape they once had. As the rectangle shrank, became more circular, it was harder to find the calm. Feeling it moving, restless, further and closer and further, feeling like he needed to move to it. Or move to where it wanted him. So he started to hit the streets with his thermos. Wandering the city as against a sandstorm. Looking for, waiting for, sometimes ignoring, the calm.

&&*&*&*

Each day he spent looking for the calm. Each day it seemed to become less attainable. He was meditating now more than looking, or at least dedicated to thinking about meditating (he could never quite clear his mind of thought, but some days, time seemed less material, seemed to pass quicker and with less coarseness) on one of the eighty-one tenets of the Tao each day. This helped. Seemed to bring the calm a step closer.

"One:
The Tao that can be told is not the eternal Tao.
The name that can be named is not the eternal name.
The nameless is the beginning of heaven and earth.
The named is the Mother of Ten Thousand Things.
Ever desireless, one can see the mystery.
Ever desiring, one can see the manifestations.
These two spring from the same source but differ in name;
this appears as darkness.
Darkness within darkness.
The gate to all mystery."

Some of the things he read seemed over-simple. Some of the teachings shortsighted or flawed. But he was was not looking for something to agree with in every letter, just something to get him closer. So he thought about the things that rubbed him wrong, deciding it was better to be thinking about them than not, and better still to not be thinking at all. One day, when the time came to descend the staircase to open the shop, he decided not to, and instead collected all the bags of rice, all the boxes of tea, from the shelves and the storage room, taking them up the stairs and packing them into the cupboards around the kitchen. The supplying done, he headed to the bank. Moving from teller to manager to supervisor, jumping through all the hoops, signing all the forms, to have all his assets released in cash.

They told him it would take several days which he spent cleaning the apartment, signing over the car title to the aggressive charity volunteer, and overall arranging things for his impending exile.

When the bank called he headed straight over, collecting what was never really his, and returning to the apartment, placed a fortune out of sight in the bedroom. It was night. He must have slept soundly for some time. Wind gushing with the noise of falling sand, something stiff creaking, something limp whipping against the building. He lit the stove to brew a kettle, smelling the flame catch its breath running a ring of dancing gaseous tongues around the burner. He sat in the room with the calm. Waiting for nothing. Knowing there was now back then, and the future is unwritten but it's just becoming the now which is becoming the back then, which will have its own resurgence when something from back then becomes part of the now, and someone will try to predict the future based on how the back then affected the now, and he couldn't try to be in the moment because the moment was only becoming the past, so he just was, unwaiting.

(*(*(*(*)*)*)*)*)

He sat on the floor for most of the eighty-one days. Leaving the door closed to the shop and relegating himself to the apartment. He paid no bills. Lived on the stockpiled rice and tea. Read the Tao Te Ching. Slept on the floor, meditating on one principle of the text each day. At the end of the 81 days he placed a table in the middle of the room upon which he stacked all the money. Dressing in now-baggy clothes and coat he walked out onto the familiar street, lost in the difference of it, and headed toward the harbor where the sun would set on another day and him waiting for it. Waiting with the calm he was taking with him. The calm that came from the usefulness of the empty space.

He had been on the bench for hours. Sleeping after the long walk to the harbor, after he felt the sun warm steady floating all around, settling on and softening his bench.

He woke to his side of the world taking leave of the day, extinguishing the last distorted tip of yolk in the black mass of beyond the bay. He poured some tea from the thermos. "He's alive mommy" a little girl swinging legs excited on a cross-the-way bench, mother trying to shush, to hold her in place.

Anogatchi pulls at the jacket and settles deeper into its warm swaddling comfort. The little girl in conference now with the mother, Anogatchi can see them exchange something, sees the pretty, soft sunken eyes of the woman smile as the little girl rushes forward, stopping with a gravel grating beneath her sneakered feet and presenting the frail man with a thick unblemished rose. In accepting it, he felt himself go weightless, and he watched from a distance as he got up and walked west, into the bay, at first the silhouette of a man parting the sun, then smaller and smaller, disappearing, into the glow.

—— More books from Neon Burrito Publishing ——

1 A collection of three poetry books by Morgan and Shawn

2 A novel by Morgan, autofiction

3 A novella by Shawn, autofiction

4 A poetry book by Shawn and Alessandra Rizzotti w/bonus grandmother appearance

5 A novelette by Shawn about becoming himself

**Basic
Mutant
Psychosis:
Annals
of Los
Angeles
2014-2016**

Stuck in an Elevator Between the 12th & 14th Floors of an Apartment Building on Rossmore

a Novel   by Morgan Drolet

Everything Within

AUTOMANIFEST

SHAWN
SULLIVAN